The Blemished Rose

PROLOGUE

Quietly he slipped down the hall. His bare feet didn't make a sound on the carpeted floor. Peeking through the doorway, he watched. This was his favorite part of the day; it always brought him warmth to see the tenderness on display in that room.

She kissed the soft, golden crown of her daughter's head as she closed the blue cover. The familiar grin looked back at her from the face of the cat, his red and white top hat leaning just a bit, his hands folded knowingly in front of him.

A sleepy voice brought her out of her melancholy.

"Read it again mommy."

She smiled. As often as they played this game, neither grew tired of it.

"How about a different story?" She suggested.

"I like this one." Came the plea.

"I think you'll like this one."

For this story, there was no book. It was all from within her mind. Snuggling the little girl tighter, she closed her eyes and began.

Once upon a time, in a land far beyond the misty moon, in a world even more magnificently beautiful than our own, there lived a mighty King. He was a King, not because a dusty piece of paper said so, but because he had earned the honor, fighting in great battles against evil and injustice. He was strong and gallant. The blade of his sword was razor sharp, and his swing was firm and true. Yet, despite his brave and fearsome reputation, he was known most for his gentle hand, and his ability to bring to life the most beautiful things. Working with gentle hands, he grew beautiful plants and trees; flowers and fruits. Known far and wide as the Master Gardener, he was the keeper of an exquisite and expansive garden of the most beautiful things in the world.

As he walked through the garden, dewdrops glistened in the morning light, reflecting the radiance of dawn like a sprinkling of diamond dust upon the leaves and blades of grass. Stillness hung in the air, and a hush fell over the land, for even the wild things grew quiet when the Master Gardener was near.

There in the garden, he worked to bring to life incredibly beautiful things. He was happy when he was in his garden; gardening was his favorite pastime, and the plants, and bushes, and trees were just as happy to see him. Wherever he walked the green leaves lifted up from the ground, the young buds unfurled their soft petals and opened their sleepy faces, all for just a moment of the master's love and attention.

Moving through the garden, he worked tirelessly. He was patient and caring; and he paid attention to even the smallest detail. There was much to do in such a large and beautiful garden, but the work he loved above all was beginning new life. With a calm and gentle nature, he lovingly helped his young plants to grow, enjoying the beauty of their existence, speaking to them; telling them how much they meant to him, and feeling how much they loved him back.

He stopped to look at his latest creation. He held the small plant within his hand, a cutting from a perfect bush. It had been carefully taken, and gently cared for until it could grow on its own. It was beautiful in every way. He gently set it aside and began preparing the ground where it would grow to be a rich and lovely rose bush.

The smell of the dark rich soil lifted up to his nose as the Master Gardener gently turned it over and over with his small spade, preparing the ground to receiving the thread-like roots which would feed the young plant. With each turn of the spade, he lifted and loosened the soil, breaking apart the clumps to form a dark, moist, powdery substance. The tenacious tentacles which formed the roots of weeds and grasses were carefully removed from the soil, along with rocks and other foreign objects. Into the soil, he mixed food which would help the plant to grow.

With great attention to detail, the plant was prepared; he spread and separated its roots. With great glee in his heart, the gardener replaced the soil, covering the roots and firmly holding the stem so that its top pointed toward the sun. Finally, the gardener offered a drink of water, pure and clear to the young plant. Then he stood back and gazed at his work with a look of satisfaction, pleased with the fruit of his labor.

The Birth of the Rose

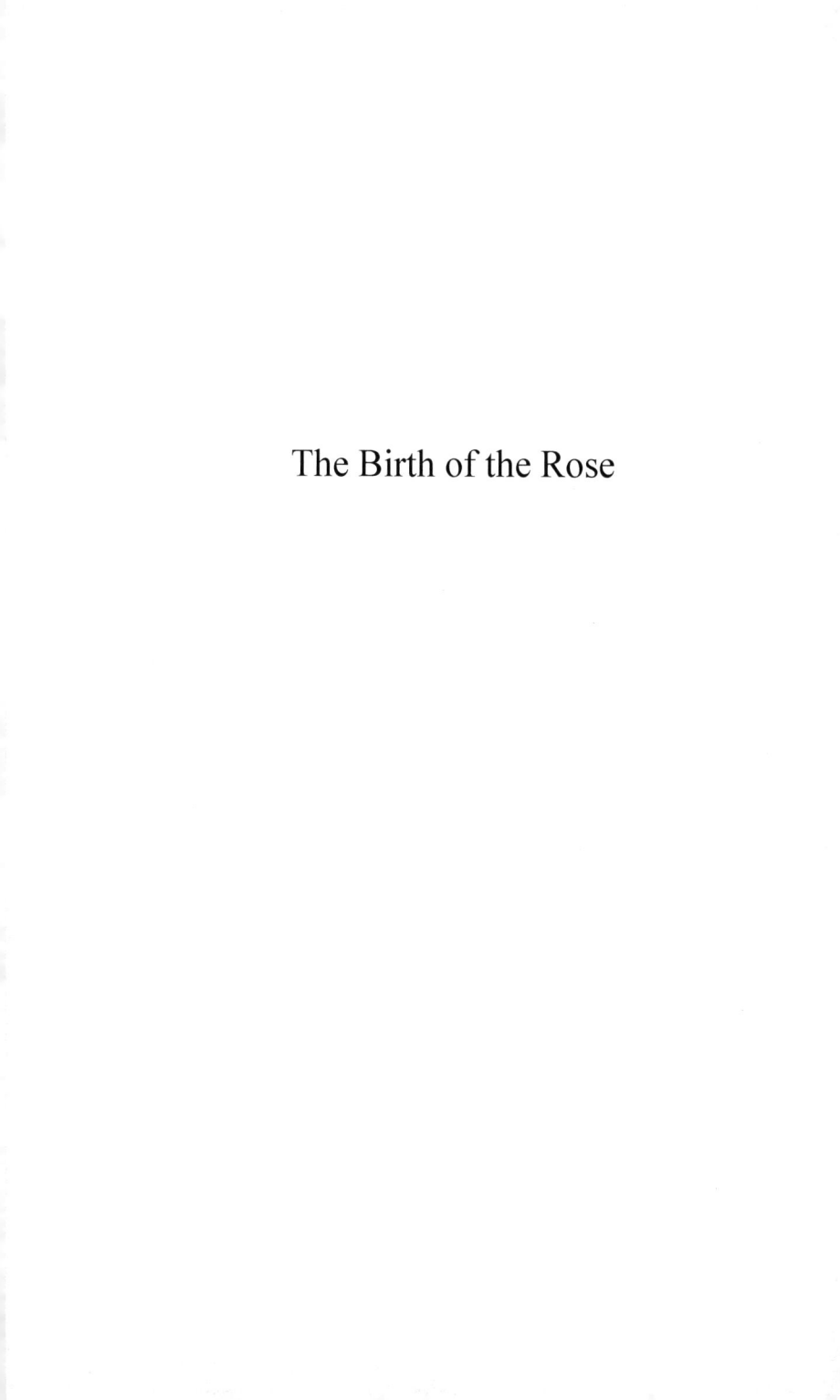

One

"Labor!" Darcy shouted. "I'm in labor!" Her shouts were directed at her husband, Dan, who was seated in his office on the other end of the phone connection. The reception was terrible and in her frantic state, she naturally reacted by raising her voice to make sure he understood.

"These cordless phones are a pain in the neck." She mumbled to herself while she tried to decipher what he was saying. Between every other word the crackle of static blared back at her. She looked at the phone in her hand and shook it, not knowing if it would help or not, but making her feel better in the process. If she didn't need it so bad at the moment, she might have flung it across the room. Replacing it to her ear, her eyes narrowed into a squint, showing the concentration upon her face while she listened intently, trying to understand his questions.

"No."

She shook her head as she answered, not thinking about the fact that he couldn't see her do it, and then she felt stupid for it afterward.

"They aren't that close yet, just head out as soon as you can. Don't speed or anything, the hospital bill is going to cost us enough, we don't need to pay a speeding ticket on top of it."

He said something else, but she couldn't make it out, and, since she felt another contraction on its way, decided to end the conversation herself.

"Okay, I'll see you in a little while. I love you. Bye."

Darcy pushed the button on the phone, staring at the receiver with a disgusted look on her face. Then she slammed it down on its base, muttering to herself about how they didn't make things like they used to.

She sat down on the couch to let the pain subside, her knees lifting automatically as the contraction met its crescendo. She felt a small amount of sweat break out on her upper lip as it reached its very peak. When it had passed, she caught her breath and dropped her feet to the floor, struggling to stand. Sometimes she felt like a turtle lying on its back, its legs flinging into the air, grabbing at the nothingness above it, anxious to roll into a position which might allow it control over its own body.

This was her first pregnancy, and it was becoming convincingly obvious she needed to give the big family dream a little more thought. Though she hadn't been plagued by the excessive nausea many women had in their early stages, the discomfort of the past few months was disheartening. She couldn't remember what it was like to look down and see the floor. She'd discovered a significant flaw in the theory of evolution and felt convinced she could disprove its relevance based on the fact that pregnant women had never developed feelers on their feet. No matter how often she looked ahead to see where the obstacles were her toes always seemed to find something to ram into, sending pain shooting through the abused appendage. She hadn't seen her toes in weeks and was convinced by now they were twisted like pretzels.

On top of all that, she felt like she was carrying around a bag of sand, tied just below her midsection. Her thighs rubbed together when she waddled along. She could feel the beads of sweat develop, and soon she was all chapped with a heat rash in the most uncomfortable of spots. And the pressure; the pressure pushing down upon her bladder was so intense she felt for sure at any moment she would explode.

She had grown increasingly self-conscious, and she was easily embarrassed when her thoughts turned to her body. When Dan reached out to touch her breasts in a playful manner, she recoiled at the tenderness of the tissue. He just didn't understand it wasn't easy to feel sexy when you were this uncomfortable. She knew he was only trying to show his affection, but she still found herself growing angry with him, just the same. Her patience had been at an all time low, and she found irritability making its way to the surface more and more frequently.

When she had successfully lifted her turtle shell from the sofa, she waddled into the bedroom to gather her things. Except for the personal items she used each day -- her make-up, toothbrush, hairbrush, and contact case -- her bag had been packed for a couple of weeks. Still she reviewed it once again, just in case. Once she was sure everything seemed to be in order, she stepped into the bathroom to collect the last few items.

She was just turning around to head back into the bedroom, when another contraction began. It was definitely stronger than the last one. She stared at the second hand on her watch, counting off the ticks until it at last subsided. It had lasted about twelve seconds longer, and she began to wonder if she had done the right thing by urging Dan not to hurry. She stood to go to the phone, and felt a sudden release of pressure, and a warm trickle down her legs, and a panic started to rise within her as she realized her water had just broke.

Grabbing up the phone, and willing herself to keep calm, she dialed his number at the office. She hoped he had already left. It was a thirty-minute commute, and she was worried he might not make it in time. When his voice came on the other end of the line her heart sunk. He could hear the nervousness in her voice as she explained what had happened.

"Okay, sweetheart, just stay calm. I can't get there quick enough, and I don't think you should drive. Is Sherri at home?"

Sherri was their neighbor next door. Darcy shook her head, once again forgetting he was unable to see it. Then she forced out a reply.

"No, Sherri had to take the twins to the dentist this morning."

She heard him take a deep breath before he replied.

"Then you'll just have to call an ambulance. I'll leave right now and meet you at the hospital."

Anxiousness was pressing in upon her.

"No, I want you to go with me. I don't want to have my baby in an ambulance."

He could hear the quiver in her voice, and he knew she was crying.

"Honey, you can't wait for me. It'll take too long. I'll meet you at the hospital. Everything will be okay. Just hang up, and call the ambulance."

Another contraction hit her, and she clinched her teeth. Realization hit her quickly and she knew if she didn't do something fast, she was going to have the baby there at home, all alone. Sweat broke out upon her brow; in fact she was sweaty all over now, but cold.

"Okay! Okay!" She was shouting now, but she couldn't help it. "Just hurry, Dan. I want you there."

When he hung up, she got a dial tone and dialed 911.

It was a quick labor, and Dan had not made it to her side in time to be part of the experience. There was a point, when the contractions were the hardest, when she just wanted him there so she could shout out all of her pain at him, but now it was over, and in her arms she held the most beautiful little girl to ever grace the face of the earth, and those thoughts had disappeared. She couldn't stop looking at her, counting her fingers, touching her skin, running her finger over the fine strands of blonde hair.

She couldn't wait to show her to Dan. He would be so happy. He had been hoping for a little girl. He'd said as much just a few days before.

"I never had a little sister, but I always wished I had. My best friend had a little sister. They fought like cats and dogs. I never really understood that. Mike and I didn't fight that much, maybe it was the age difference. Mike's almost ten years older than me, so he kind of took care of me, and showed me the ropes."

She smiled as he talked to her. Darcy always liked to listen to Dan talk. Once he got started he just seemed to ramble on, and the sound of his voice was so relaxing she often found herself growing sleepy as he spoke. When he realized she was asleep he would always stop talking, and she'd stir enough to tell him she was still listening.

"So, sounds like you pretty much have your heart set on a girl. What if it turns out the other way? Are you going to be disappointed?

He shook his head.

"No, I hope it's a girl, but I'm sure I'll be just as happy if it's a boy. There will be a lot of things we can do together, but I won't buy the baseball mitt until we know for sure."

Looking down at the little girl in her arms, Darcy thought, "It better be a pink mitt, Dan."

Though she was tired from her ordeal, it was amazing how quickly the pain and memory of labor had disappeared when they placed the baby in her arms. Except for allowing them to clean her up, Darcy had refused to let the nurses take her little girl away. When the nurse came in asking about a name for the birth certificate, she had put her off by asking if they could wait until the father arrived. Dan had missed the birth, but she wanted to be sure he was there when they finally gave the baby a name.

After laying eyes on her child, Darcy had made her choice. She wanted to call the baby Elina, after the creamy yellow rose which grew in her mother's garden. The name seemed appropriate enough given her blonde hair, and her rose-petal-soft skin, but just to be sure, she wanted to see what Dan thought about it. They'd talked over several names during the last nine months and hadn't settled on any in particular. She wondered what was keeping Dan. She glanced at the clock on the wall. It wasn't quite rush hour yet, but she supposed traffic could still be bad.

Darcy tilted her head down, and kissed the top of the baby's head. Her hair was soft against Darcy's lips, and she could smell the baby shampoo the nurses had used to wash her up after the birth. She thought back to the night when they had conceived her. It was an incredible moment, and though they had tried months before, she knew, at that moment, it would work that time.

Both Darcy and Dan had wanted children from the beginning. In fact, they had talked about it many times while they were going together. After they were engaged, they had both agreed, however, it wasn't practical to bring a baby into a family that wasn't financially prepared. They set in place some ground rules, to insure they were financially secure before trying to have the baby.

They had been married nearly four years, before they tried the first time, and they were on a strong financial footing. The only bills they had were the house and the mini van. Another car was paid for in full, and that was the one that Dan used to commute back and forth to work. It wasn't much, but it was economical and served the purpose.

They were unsuccessful the first few months they had tried to conceive, but then it took. That one ended up in a miscarriage which took a strong emotional toll on Darcy. She was only three months along, but it hurt just the same. One day she was pregnant, and the next day she wasn't. According to the doctor, there was no way to know just what went wrong.

"Sometimes these things just happen, and we just have to trust there was a reason. Maybe there was something wrong with the fetus. We just don't know."

She had trouble accepting his words at first, even though they had been delivered with care and consideration. Later, after she had put a little time and thought between herself and the event, she knew the doctor was probably right.

After about six months, they tried in earnest once again, and it took another couple of months before anything happened. But that night, after their love making had ended, and she was still resting in its glow, Dan asleep at her side, a feeling, no, more than a feeling, something in her heart told her, it would all turn out right this time. She was even pretty sure of the baby's sex at that time, though she tried not to allow herself to come to expect it.

Her pregnancy had taken place without a hitch, right up until labor. She still couldn't believe it had happened without Dan at her side. She had always expected he would be there. He had even, without complaint, participated in the Lamaze' classes she enrolled them in a few months ago. He was the life of the group, taking everything seriously, but not missing an opportunity for a laugh. He would talk to her stomach, and tell it to listen up, and do as the teacher told her.

Dan had been nearly as involved in the birth experience as she had. The excitement in his eyes when he had first felt the baby move made him look like a little boy. And when he felt the thumps of the baby kicking, he started calling Darcy his little soccer mom.

"She's gonna punch right through the wall. There won't be any reason to go into labor, she'll just come straight on out."

He'd said that one night, while they lay in bed together watching the usual bedtime commotion going on inside of her.

"Eeww. Now you're giving me images from Alien. Don't do that."

She paused.

"How do you know it's a she?" Darcy asked with a wry smile.

He stumbled just a bit.

"Uh, I don't, but I just don't feel comfortable saying 'it' all of the time."

Darcy loved the way he would run his hands gently over her belly, and talk softly to the baby inside. Dan had never once led her to feel he was at all disappointed that her shape had changed with the experience. She had gained twenty pounds over the last nine months, but Dan never teased or taunted her over it. He had even understood when in the later months she felt too uncomfortable to continue with sex.

"You have a great dad," she said quietly to the bundle in her arms. "He's going to be so excited to see you. I know you both are going to be real close."

Dan and Darcy had met at a party back in college. He was a bright young business student in his third year, she a freshman athlete on a track scholarship. He planned on going into sales, and she knew instantly he would be successful. He won her over with his ability to make conversation seem sincere and comfortable. He had a fantastic smile, and the careful way he would listen to her when she was talking just pushed it over the top. His eyes would lock on, and he seemed to absorb her every word. When he asked her to get a cup of coffee with him after the party ended, she searched for a reason to say no, trying not to be easily won, but she simply couldn't find one. They quickly became an item.

After he graduated, he got a job there in Stillwater, and waited patiently for her to finish school. Then they moved to Denton. It was the perfect place for them; not quite in the heart of the big city, yet close enough for Dan to commute to his job with a pharmaceutical firm on the outskirts of Dallas. Dan's career had grown even faster than the two of them expected, and he quickly moved from a field rep to vice president of the sales department.

Now they had a darling little girl. What more could they hope for? Maybe a couple more kids. She raised her brow. A few hours ago that was almost out of the question, but now…she could see herself ferrying kids around from ballet, to soccer, to music lessons. The thought made her smile.

There was a knock at the door and she sat up in the bed, expecting Dan, but it was just a nurse. Then she glanced again.

It was in that one brief instant, when she had taken the time for a second glance at the door, Darcy Pearson's world changed forever. The joyous feelings, in which she had been swimming just moments before, disappeared into a hollow abyss. She felt the lump form in her throat, and the hollow pit swell up inside of her, her heart sinking into its depths, as she looked up into the eyes of the highway patrol officer who stood in the doorway behind the nurse. At his side was the hospital Chaplin. She felt the tears begin to trickle down her cheeks, even before the thoughts had settled in her mind. Her lips began to quiver as she formed the words which seemed to catch in her throat.

"Dan's not coming, is he?"

The officer just shook his head, slowly. His face was stoic and unemotional, but in his eyes she could see the tears he held back. She could tell he was struggling with having to deliver news like this to a new mother, her infant not even two hours old. The Chaplin moved over to her side and took her hand. The nurse reached out, lifting the baby from her arms. And then, Darcy Pearson, widowed mother of one, burst, the sudden burden of losing the father of her child, becoming too much for her to contain.

Two

The funeral was held two days after Darcy and Elina were released from the hospital. Across the large sanctuary, the pews were filled to capacity. Dan was loved and respected by a great number of people including friends, co-workers and clients. The heavy somberness hung in the air, and when she was lead to the front, everyone's eyes were transfixed on the young mother, dressed in black, holding her newborn close at her breast.

She knew their thoughts, and even in her grief, was angry at being the subject of their pity. She could feel their eyes upon her, and knew they whispered among themselves.

"Poor girl, and her with that new baby to raise."

"They said he was rushing to the hospital when it happened."

"It's such a shame the baby never got to know her father."

"Can't see how she keeps her composure. I'd be a wreck."

Darcy Pearson, widow and mother, stared ahead, eyes unwavering, looking on at the closed casket of her one true love, and the father of her child. She wasn't about to give them the satisfaction of seeing her breakdown. She had done enough of that the past few days, and if it was to happen again, it would happen in her own home, behind closed doors, where she could be alone in her sorrow.

Besides, she had to be strong now. She was the only one Elina had left. They would make it. Somehow, they would make it. She told herself this time and again, but whenever she thought of life without Dan, the emptiness of the thought seemed to suck the life right out of her. It was better if she didn't think about it, so she put up a strong front, and held her head up to listen to the minister.

"Dan Pearson was a loving and affectionate man. His passing offers much sorrow, but just as we gather here to mourn the passing of one life, in the midst of our sorrow, a new life takes hold. Elina Danielle Pearson was born the day her father died. We must remember, though life often delivers us burdens of grief which seem too much to bear, just so God offers blessings of gladness and joy. I am sure in the days to come, Darcy, you will find in Elina blessings beyond measure, blessings which allow you some comfort in your moment of grief."

So, there it was. It was so easy to say. The same God who had allowed Dan to die, the same God who had her allowed to face a world alone, was given credit for the blessing of this new life. It was a thought she couldn't accept, at least not right now. How could she reach out to this God who had just taken so much away from her, from both of them? She was angry, and there was only one place to direct that anger.

At the end of the service, when everyone else had been ushered out of the room, Darcy stepped toward the casket. Even the light reflecting off the polished finish of the casket irritated her. It was a despicable object; one which would carry all that was left of Dan away from her to be buried in the dirt. On the top of the oak vessel containing the remains of her love, a large spray of yellow roses spread out to embrace what was left. With Elina held against her in one arm, she reached out for one of the yellow buds. As she gently caressed its tender petals, she silently told Dan goodbye. Her eyes welled up with tears, building, eager to overflow, but holding back like liquid against the rim of a glass, unable to break the bonds of surface tension. With all her will, she fought them back.

In the days and months which followed, Darcy found it was all she could do to get up out of bed and feed Elina. Each time she thought of Dan, that same hollow, empty ache rose up within her. She still found it hard to believe he was gone, and she found herself expecting to see him or to hear his voice; at six o'clock when he would normally arrive home from work; in the middle of the night when she turned over toward where he slept; at noon, when he would have called her just to see how her day was going. And yet, he was not there. He was not there to hold her and warm her, and it left her feeling alone and lost, like a piece of her soul had disappeared.

Friends tried to get her out of the house. They invited her to dinner. They stopped by to check on her. Her family called frequently. She pushed them away. She pushed them all away. They couldn't help her. They couldn't bring Dan back. No one could. He was gone forever and so were their hopes and dreams of a life together. Gone were the dreams of a big family, gone was the warm feelings she got when he looked into her eyes.

Sometimes she would find herself sitting and staring at his picture, the one that was taken the day he had been promoted to vice president. In her mind she would try to remember every intricate detail of his being, the touch of his skin, the sound of his voice, the scent he left on her pillow. She would run her finger over the surface of the paper, tracing his outline, willing it back to life. Her eyes would fix on his smile, and she would try to remember his laugh. Then she would feel her emptiness, and sink deeper into her despair.

That's exactly what she was doing when Elina began to cry that morning. She felt herself grow angry for the interruption. It was her time; her time with Dan, and the baby should be asleep anyway. She sat there a little longer, hoping Elina would just go back to sleep, but she didn't. Her cries became stronger, and then they turned into wails, and Darcy allowed the anger to build up within her, until she finally burst up from the bed to go to Elina's room.

It was nearly one o'clock in the afternoon, but the shades were drawn, and the house was dark. She stumbled over a pile of discarded clothes and nearly fell. It only served to increase her frustration, and by the time she reached Elina's crib, it had nearly consumed her. She wanted to pick her up and shake her, to make her stop that infernal crying. She wanted her to stop interrupting her and calling her at all hours of the night and day.

She lifted the child from her crib, and held Elina out before her, her arms extended, the anger seething within her. Then in the only light of the room, a sliver of brightness peeking from around the drawn shade, she saw

Elina's face and her anger dissolved in shame. For there, looking back at her was Dan's sweet smile. And reality hit her squarely in the chest. She felt ashamed, and horrified. How could she have allowed herself to slip so far into the abyss?

Darcy looked around her. The room was in disarray. There were clothes scattered and strewn about. The can beside the crib was full of discarded diapers, and bottles littered the top of the changing table. She looked back at Elina, dressed only in a diaper, and she felt selfish. For in her grief, she had deprived her daughter of the attention she so desperately needed. She had neglected to offer her the warmth of her love. In the wake of Dan's death, she had been wasting time away staring at images upon paper, rekindling lost memories, and forsaking the only real part of Dan which was left.

She pulled her baby close to her breast, feeling the warmth of Dan's love in that living, breathing piece of him, that cutting from his soul which had become a life of its own, and then Darcy Pearson wept. She wept for the loss of the love of her life, and she wept for the blessing of Dan's constant reminder in the form of his little girl, the little girl who held his smile, and would, no doubt, share at least a portion of his personality. And through her grief, despite her grief, she offered up thanks to a God above who had, before taking her love away, left her this little, warm reminder that it would always be with her.

Getting her life back together wasn't easy. There were times when she wanted to slip back into that cocoon she had created for herself. The burden of caring for her baby, and dealing with her grief sometimes overwhelmed her, but she learned to use those moments to release her sorrow, rather than letting it build into anger. She still cried, she cried often, but somehow by allowing the tears to flow, she was able to release herself from the clutches of despair.

Over time the tears, were fewer and, with Elina around, she found more and more reasons to smile. There were new things they discovered about each other every day. Elina was growing and crawling. Then she was standing and walking. Darcy would sit with her and show her pictures of two of them, she and Dan, together. She was determined, though he was not there to see her, Elina would know her father. Elina would know her daddy was kind and compassionate; she would find ways to teach her that he was witty and charming, and she constantly reminded her that he would have loved her with all his heart, though he had never seen her with his own eyes.

Six months after Dan's death their financial situation began to press in upon the little family of mother and daughter. Darcy found it necessary to go back to work. She applied for, and was accepted to a job as a P.E. coach with an elementary school. With the twins in school, her neighbor, Sherri, consented to taking care of Elina while she worked. Darcy immersed herself in her work, and in sharing her evenings with Elina. It wasn't as good as being with her all day, but it was workable, and it did allow her to occupy her thoughts. Besides, working with the elementary children offered her even more reasons to smile.

Days turned into months, months turned into years, and the baby who had Dan's smile, grew into a young girl. Her bright smile never ceased to win over her mother's heart. Her sky-blue eyes sparkled with wonder and energy. Her yellow-blonde hair fell over her dainty little shoulders in wavy curls. She learned quickly, and Darcy was ever amazed at her ability to carry on a conversation. She supposed it was because they talked so much, mother and daughter. She seemed to pick up on things which were beyond other children her age.

When Elina was six years old, she surprised Darcy with the question she had never stopped to ponder herself. The two had spent the day shopping at the mall. Elina's inquiry seemed to come out of the blue.

"Mommy, will I ever have another Daddy?"

Darcy wasn't sure exactly how to respond. Ever since Dan's death, she had been so caught up in teaching her daughter to appreciate the daddy who had given her his smile, she hadn't stopped to think about the possibility of meeting someone else. There had been a few times when she'd felt attracted to someone, but she pushed those feelings aside, knowing she needed to focus all of her attention on Elina, not on herself. Besides, no one could replace Dan.

"I don't know, honey. Why do you ask?"

Elina held her head down, looking at the floor. She was obviously not sure she should have asked the question and she was reluctant to explain why. It always amazed Darcy how grown up she could be sometimes, and she liked to think of her as a little person, rather than as just a child. Sensing her discomfort, Darcy attempted to ease her concerns.

"It's okay, sweetheart. You can tell mommy anything. You don't have to be embarrassed or afraid."

Elina's eyes rose up cautiously. "I just sometimes wish I had a daddy who could do things with me, like other kids. Not just a picture daddy."

Her words brought back the painful reminders that Dan would never be around to do those things father's and daughters do, and his absence would always leave a void in Elina's life, as well as her own. Darcy tried to fill the gaps, but she knew eventually Elina would feel the pressure of her peers and realize there was something different about their situation. She couldn't suppress the discomforting feeling in her throat, but she found a way to speak past its growing presence.

"I know it's hard not having a daddy around, but there are lots of other kids who don't have daddies and some of them don't have mommies, either. We do have each other, though, and I'll try to do anything daddy would do if he were here. All you have to do is ask me."

"I know mommy. I just wondered. Samantha said she got a new daddy, so I just wondered when I would get one."

Darcy smiled with understanding.

"I see. Well, I'm very happy for Samantha, and you should be, too, but daddies aren't something you just go pick out at the store. It's kind of complicated to explain. Maybe, someday, if I meet someone I think would make a good daddy for you and me, then we'll have a new daddy, but until then, I guess it's just you and me, Pumpkin. Is that okay?"

Elina nodded. Darcy squatted down to look her in the eyes. Holding her shoulders, she smiled and encouraged her daughter.

"I think we make a pretty good team. I think Daddy would be proud of us, don't you?"

At that Elina smiled in agreement.

Darcy stood up and took her hand. For a while they walked hand in hand around the mall, each lost in their thoughts, until Darcy broke the silence.

"How about some ice cream?"

Elina gave her a wide approving grin.
"Can I have chocolate? It's my favorite."
"Anything you like, sweetheart, anything you like."

Three

Green leaves fluttered in the breeze, as the Frisbee floated across the baby blue background. Darcy watched as her daughter ran to meet it. Her little legs moved as quickly as possible, her bare feet parting the blades of grass, her giggles trailing in the air behind her. She was a bundle of energy, and from a distance her golden curls were like rays of sunlight forming a halo around her head.

The park was a reward for the review she had gotten from her first grade teacher.

"This little girl is as sharp as a tack. She catches on so quickly to everything. If she keeps this up we may have to consider moving her into an advanced class."

Darcy beamed with the news.

"Just for that little girl, we are going to have to find something special to do this weekend."

"Can we go to the zoo, and then to the park?" She asked with excitement.

"The zoo and the park? Hmm. Is that where they have all of those animals?"

"Yeah, it's my favorite."

"Let's see. I just happen to have two tickets to the zoo right here in my purse." Her mother teased.

"Yay! Can we go Mommy? Can we?"

Darcy pretended to be thinking.

"Oh, I guess."

Elina loved the zoo. She had to see everything. Darcy bought her one of those disposable cameras and she had taken most of the pictures within the first fifteen minutes.

"You need to slow down on the pictures sweetheart. You're going to use up all of your film before you even get to the elephants."

"I just don't want to miss anything, mommy."

"Well, next time we walk by a gift stand maybe we can get another one."

The hippos were her favorites. It took all of Darcy's powers of persuasion to pull her away from them. She was so engrossed in their playful romps; she didn't seem to hear a word her mother was saying.

"I was thinking about letting you take ballet this year. How would you like that?"

Darcy waited for her reply.

"Elina? Did you hear me?"

She turned her head.

"What mommy?"

"I said I was thinking about letting you take ballet this year. Would you like to do that?"

She smiled.

"Oh, yes mommy."

After the zoo, they had stopped for a picnic in the park. The afternoon had been relatively mild, the green grass so inviting, soon both mother and daughter had discarded their shoes and began a playful game of tag.

When the man at the table next to them had offered to let them use his Frisbee, Elina's pleading eyes had pierced her heart, and she could not find the strength to say no.

They tossed the plastic disc back and forth over and over. In the beginning Darcy spent more time chasing it as it rolled along on its edge, as Elina struggled to throw it with all of her might. Once she discovered how to make it float upon the air, the game became more exciting and Darcy tried desperately to absorb the image of her amazed young face when she saw it lifted into the baby blue sky.

When they got into the van to leave, Elina began to plead once again.

"Can we stop for ice cream?"

Darcy glanced into the mirror at her daughter.

"What do you say?"

"Please?"

"I guess, since you've been so good lately."

"Mommy, did you see that man under the tree at the park?"

"There were lots of people under trees at the park. Which one?"

"That one man by himself. He looked so lonely. He looked like that picture of daddy."

"Which picture of daddy?" She asked glancing back once again.

Darcy loved to watch her daughter as she talked. She was so animated, using her hands as gestures, just the way Dan had. When they had first started dating she use to kid him that he wouldn't be able to say a word if someone tied his hands still. Elina had somehow inherited that trait.

"The picture of daddy when you were in the mountains. The one under the big pine tree."

"Oh. No, I didn't see that man."

"I think he wanted to talk to me."

"What makes you think that?"

The thought of a strange man talking with her six year old bothered her. She'd heard so many stories in the news about child abductors; it was scary.

"He kept waving at me."

"Did you talk to the man?"

"No, he was a stranger and you told me not to talk with strangers."

She was relieved; at least some of her instructions had made an impact.

"That's right. You don't talk to strangers."

"But I'm sure he was just lonely."

Darcy countered. "That doesn't matter."

"I know mommy, but he looked like daddy."

"Well, we both know it wasn't daddy. Daddy isn't here anymore."

Elina was quiet a moment before she spoke.

"I wish he was here."

"Me too." Darcy replied. Then she added, "But we do okay, right? Girlfriends forever, right?"

"Yep, that's right mommy." Then she added, "But someday I might get a new daddy, right?"

"Maybe someday."

Elina was quiet the rest of the way home. Darcy too was lost in thought. It was becoming more and more evident that Elina was ready to move on with her life. Her daughter was willing to accept another daddy into her life, but was she?

Four

There is a place in the heart which cries out to be acknowledged. Sometimes it whispers gently in the quiet of night, an echo falling softly, tenderly upon the senses, wearing them down slowly as the placid flow of a meandering stream changes the landscape over the courses of time. At other times it screams out like the thunderous rage of a river, fed by the drip, drip, drip of a spring thaw, flooding the soul, overflowing its boundaries, until it consumes all in its path. Whether as breathily as a whisper, or as vociferous as a scream, it commands notice, demands acknowledgment, of its lonely existence, of its insatiable need for companionship.

Darcy Pearson heard the call, felt the lonely agony within her. There was a growing need, unnoticed in the wake of Dan's passing or in the early stages of Elina's life, yet it was there all along, the separation of one human soul from another to which it might cling, and share, and love. A feeling she could ignore for a period of time until it developed and split, developed and split, multiplying in intensity, until it pressed upon her heart, touching the senses which had been dulled by pain and loss.

Of course she tried to dismiss it by explaining it away and claiming it as impossible. She used Elina as her excuse, telling herself she should offer Elina her undivided attention; reminding herself there wasn't time in her life for another person. She beat it away with a stick of guilt, reprimanding the voice for trying to make her forget Dan. Yet it was there and it gnawed at her. Darcy secretly wondered to herself when or if she would feel comfortable accepting the affections of another man.

The evening after her conversation with Elina, lying in bed alone, she replayed Elina's questions. She felt sadness at the thought that her daughter felt something missing in her life. She had tried so desperately to fill any void Dan's absence had left, but she knew there would always be things mothers and daughters did differently than fathers and daughters.

Elina would learn to cope, eventually, she knew this, but how would it affect her? What thoughts and emotions would be influenced by being the child of a single parent? How would Elina choose to compensate for this missing element in her life? Those were the things which concerned Darcy.

As for her, there were moments in which Darcy felt the ache, a longing for the warmth of another person. Most often it began with thoughts of Dan, but it slowly evolved into something vague and undefined. Feelings of loneliness twisted and distorted until they ignited something deep within her, something she usually fought to control.

The house was quiet and Elina had long since ended her restless fight against sleep in her room down the hall.

The day was busy, filled with shopping, and though she resisted, she was obviously wore out. Darcy was alone now, alone with her thoughts and the tantalizing feelings growing within her, alone to sort it all out and make sense of the confusion which had become her life.

Just when she had seemed to get everything together, just when she had built a bridge across the chasm which had been created by Dan's death, she now faced a point in her life when she had to do it all over again. She knew she couldn't *just* go on, she couldn't pretend she never felt alone or that it didn't matter there was no one in her life to fill the vacant spot, or in her bed to offer the completion of another soul to bind with hers. She knew it was simply not enough to go on, it was necessary to do more. She couldn't continue to deny herself the possibility of happiness, the happiness which had been stripped from her.

It was that thought, that desire for companionship, which prompted her to finally do what she thought she had done six years earlier. Rising from her bed, she crossed the room and lit a candle. With light from the candle in her hand flickering around the room, casting a yellow glow upon the walls, she made her way determinedly across the room.

She felt the coolness of the hardwood floor on the bottoms of her bare feet, another reminder of Dan. He had insisted on leaving the hardwood uncovered. Ever the romantic, Dan loved the contrast of the dark wood floors against the Victorian style paper with which they had covered the walls. While on their honeymoon in Fredericksburg, they had visited a quaint little bed and breakfast and they both fell in love with the décor. When they set about looking for a home, it was the images of that cottage which had the strongest influence upon their decisions.

Darcy's satin gown swished against her legs as she moved through the candlelight, her shadow casting itself against the wall. She stopped to look at the dark, giant image it created, thinking it ironic in relation to the enormity of the feelings seeming to consume her. She continued, slowly approaching the dresser, which sat in the corner of the room. The dresser was again a reminder of Dan. He had purchased it while on one of his trips. Passing an antique store, he couldn't resist the antique oak finish. On the top of the dresser she had devoted a spot to Dan's pictures and they sat there grouped together like little monuments or a shrine to a god.

Darcy gathered up the pictures and carried them over to the bed, laying them out before her. The light danced off the glass of the frames in front of her, and as she gazed at the images, her focus moved from the flickering reflection of the flame on the candle to the picture of Dan beneath the glass. For a long while she sat staring at the pictures, reliving memories as she had so often.

In her mind she could see Dan there in the park playing football with the rest of his college buddies. He was so athletic and handsome. And there was his smile as he glanced over at her sitting on the sidelines. He was a great looking guy, and any girl would have been happy to be seen with him, but that smile, that was by far the thing which got to her the most. His deep dimples seemed to pull up the corners of his mouth. Whenever they fought, which wasn't often, he would flash that smile of his and all of the cold, tense emotions just seemed to melt away. She couldn't possibly stay mad at him.

Dan was a talker; he could charm his way out of anything. He'd done it often enough with her. Just when she thought she had reached the point of no return, Dan would needle and cajole her until she was forced to smile despite herself. People just naturally liked him and they congregated towards him. His decision to join the sales market was a simple one; he was born for it.

Darcy reached out for one of the pictures on her bed. The picture in the rosewood frame was taken when they were on their honeymoon. Dan had arranged to take her sailing down by Padre Island. Once they were out on the water, he convinced the schooner captain to let him take the wheel, and she caught him on film looking smug like he was a real sailor.

The memories created warm feelings she couldn't suppress and she found herself whispering to him.

"You could be such a ham. You always found a way to make me laugh. Somehow you brought out the best in every situation."

She paused in thought.

"We had a real good time down there, didn't we Dan? I'd never seen that much water before. Remember the night we slept out on the beach? We were the only ones around. I never thought you could have convinced me to get naked out on the beach like that, but you did. It was so erotic. I had sand in places I thought was humanly impossible. Oh God, that was a beautiful night. The stars were so bright, and the moon reflecting off the water, it was just gorgeous. We built a fire, but when the breeze cooled off I thought we were going to freeze, and I told you we should go back, but you said we'd just snuggled up closer and we'd be fine. You were right. That was all I needed, just the warmth of your body against mine. Just you by my side..."

Her thoughts dangled precariously between the past and the present, swinging slowly back and forth like a pendulum, measuring the distance between the two. She fought the sorrow which threatened to eat away at her memories, yet she could feel it building within her, the sadness which seems to grow with each passing second. Still the pendulum swung, back and forth. With each swing the present came closer, it's pull stronger than those of fleeting memories, until finally it overtook her and came sweeping forth, and with the it, the loneliness, the emptiness, and the longing, followed by the tears for times which would never return. However, she felt the need to continue... to tell Dan what she had never been able to tell him before.

"That was all I needed then, and it's all I need now, but you can't be here, not that way. I know you would be, if you could, but you can't, and I can't go on trying to wish it all back. Your memory warms my heart, but the space beside me is cold."

Her eyes pooled blurring images in the room. Tears rolled down her cheeks, dripping onto the glass frame in front of her. She held her breath, struggling to keep control of her emotions and to keep her words to a whisper. While every part of her wanted to cry out, she suppressed her grief to keep from waking her little girl down the hall.

"I don't blame you, Dan. It's not your fault. And it's not my fault either. I think...I think for a long time I did blame myself... for asking you to hurry. But blaming myself didn't help. It didn't make it go away or bring you back. It just made me hate going on without you. But I have to go on. I have to go on for Elina and for me."

"She's beautiful, Dan, she really is beautiful. She has your smile. She's so bright and cheerful, just like her daddy. I hope where you are, you can watch her grow-up. Maybe you can keep a special eye on her when she is away from me, kind of like a guardian angel. She knows who you are, Dan. She knows what kind of man you were, and how much you would have loved her. I've made sure of that. We talk about you all the time. I hope when she grows up she finds a man just like you."

She was determined now. She knew what she had to say, and though part of her feared the words, and warned her against it, she knew they had to be spoken.

"Dan, I don't want to, but I've got to let you go. We have to go on, Elina and I."

She pushed past her fear.

"I thought I said goodbye once before, at your funeral, but I realize now, I never meant it. I kept trying to hang on to you. I kept trying to keep you with me, but you're gone and nothing I do can change that. I hope you understand. I'll always love you, Dan, and there will always be a part of me that belongs only to you, but I have to stop grieving for you. You're okay, but I'm not, not as long as I keep hanging on to you. We'll always have those memories, but I've got let you go. We both have our own paths to take and maybe someday in some other place, they'll cross again. I hope so. But for now, I have to say goodbye."

"It hurts to do this. I never, in all my life, ever imagined things would go this way; that there would ever be a time when I would force you away from me; or that I wouldn't want you near. And really it's not what I want to do; it's just what I have to do. I have to Dan; it's the only way. If I don't, it'll be the same as if I died with you. And even though there have been times when I wished I had, we both know that's not possible. Elina needs me, Dan, because she doesn't have you. Goodbye, Dan. Goodbye, my love."

The tears were dry now. In her heart she still felt the sorrow, but not the grief. It was like when she was a little girl and her father had been transferred. She remembered waving goodbye to her best friend, Cathy. She could see her out of the back window of the station wagon. She remembered holding her hand up until she could no longer see the image of her friend. She was sad and felt lonely, but after they had been on the road for a little while her mood recovered. Then it only hurt when she stopped to think about it and after they had moved in to their new house and she had made some new friends, it didn't hurt much at all. She felt that way now, sorrow for a time that would never be again, but relieved she had at last said goodbye.

Darcy put her finger to her lips and then pressed it against the image in front of her. Then she gathered all of the pictures, except the large one, the picture of the two of them together on the bow of the schooner. This picture she placed back upon the dresser, as a reminder of a life once lived. The others were placed in a chest in the closet, where other keepsakes were stored. They took their spot among wedding photos, high school yearbooks, and her prom dress. These were the things, the pieces of the past, she would someday offer to her daughter, but for now they were stored away, captured moments, held in a cedar time-capsule, suspended, waiting for the moment when they were needed to jog a memory or to return to a place long forgotten.

She blew out the candle and slipped under the covers of her bed. She felt exhausted, used up, but comforted to be free of the burden of guilt, and grief.

Somewhere in the moments which followed Darcy's eyes grew heavy and she slipped off to sleep, dreaming dreams of a little girl with a radiant smile; running into the open arms of a man with dimples that pulled in the corners of his mouth. He was crouched down, his knees bent, like a catcher. As Darcy looked on she saw them embrace and he kissed the top of her head. Then the man pointed at Darcy whispering in the child's ear. And back she came, back towards Darcy. He raised his hand and waved, and then he turned and walked away.

The Budding of the Rose

Five

Phillip Henning opened the door of the van, gently lifting the sleeping child from her seat. She was exhausted. They had spent the entire day at the zoo, while her mother stayed at home with the baby. They considered making it a family affair, but decided the heat would be too much for Danny. He was merely six months old, and a July afternoon in the Houston sun and humidity wasn't the place for an infant. Elina was disappointed she wouldn't get to introduce her little brother to all the animals, but she quickly recovered when her mother told her she could take pictures for both of them to see.

After the zoo, the father-daughter team stopped by Chuckee Cheese's for some pizza and games. Phillip was entertained by her scramble from game to game, her interests changing as she explored the room. She was quite good at most of them. When she finally tired of the video games and skeeball, it was off to the ice cream shop and when they eventually pulled in the driveway, she was out.

Darcy was there to meet him at the door, holding it open as he carried his precious package inside. She smiled at the image of her daughter, and followed Phillip down the hall to pull down her sheets. He gently laid her into her bed, worried she might wake. Darcy undressed her, pulled the covers over her and kissed her forehead. Then they both crept out the doorway and pulled the door closed behind them.

"She's a mess, dad. What did you let her do, roll in an ice cream factory?"

"I guess a double banana split was a bit messy for her."

Darcy nearly questioned his motives for allowing Elina to consume so much ice cream, but stopped short of voicing her thoughts. She knew Phillip was doing his best to fill the big shoes he had stepped into. Even though Elina had never met her father, to her he was the greatest guy who ever lived, and accepting someone in his place, although she had even suggested it herself at one time hadn't been easy for her. Their relationship had been fine while Darcy and Phillip dated, but after the wedding and Phillip moved in, it had been a little stormy.

Things had softened some with the birth of Danny. Elina accepted him well; in fact she doted over him all the time. She helped with his diapers, she fed him, and she kept him busy when her mother was working around the house. Elina had come to believe it was her job to show Danny the ropes, and she took her tasks quite seriously.

Phillip was apologetic.

"Aw, I know I shouldn't have let her have so many sweets, but we were having such a good time, and it's not something we do everyday."

Darcy nodded.

"So, how was the zoo?"

Phillip smiled a victorious smile.

"It was a big success. She told me about every animal in the place. I don't think the zookeepers could have offered any more information. You should have heard her when we got to the petting zoo. 'Phillip can we get a rabbit? Phillip can you buy me a sheep? I'll keep him in the back yard.' She wouldn't stop. So, I finally said okay when she asked for a snake. I figured it wouldn't take up too much room. Oh, I better go get it, it's still in the van."

Darcy's face was aghast.

"You're kidding me. Phillip Henning, you better not have a snake in that van. We are not having a snake in this house."

Her discomfort was calmed by his laughter and Darcy knew she'd been had.

"I'm just kidding, it's only a lizard."

She was on to him now, and she laughed as she threw the couch pillow at him.

"'Bout three feet long, ugly green thing."

He continued unabated, until she rose from her spot on the couch and came over to sit on his lap.

"Terrible breath. Eats mice."

She pressed her nose to his.

"Settles for flies when mice are scarce."

She kissed his forehead.

"Long tongue, long tongue."

She kissed his lips.

"Yeah, like that."

She hit him with the pillow again.

He changed the subject. "How's slugger?"

She slid off his lap and sat beside him.

"Oh, he's fine. He went to sleep just before you guys drove up."

"Did you guys have fun without us?"

Darcy smiled.

"Yeah. He wanted to stay awake to see the lizard, but I told him he could see you in the morning."

Now it was Phillip's turn to toss the pillow.

"I'm tired. I think I'll take a shower, want to join me?"

"Sorry, already had one," she teased as she stood up and walked toward the bedroom. She had that playful look on her face, the one he loved so much, her sexy look, so he decided to get in one last dig.

"Me too, but it wasn't all that refreshing coming out of the trunk of an elephant."

"Yuck."

Long after their lovemaking had ended, Darcy lay awake thinking, staring into the night. Next week was Elina's birthday and the eighth anniversary of Dan's death. She still thought about him from time to time, and when she did she could still feel a sorrow for all they had lost. But now there was Phillip, not a replacement for Dan, but someone new in her life. It was hard at first, allowing him in to that place in her heart where only Dan had visited. She dealt with feelings of betrayal, especially when Elina reacted the way she did after the wedding. It was almost hard to believe it had been eight years since she'd lost him.

She met Phillip a year and a half earlier. Sensing she needed something positive in her life, their lives, she and Elina had started attending a local church. It was pretty simple at first, just the regular Sunday morning worship service, but then she let Elina attend the Vacation Bible School program. After that she wanted to go to Sunday school each week, so Darcy started going as well. She attended the singles group, and that's where she met Phillip.

He was a striking man, thirty-five years old, the same age as her. There was just a touch of gray to his black hair, kind of a peppering in the temples. Overall, he was bigger than Dan and, had he shared a different demeanor, he could have been menacing. He had a large barrel chest, and when he hugged her, he reminded her of a bear. His brown eyes were calm, dark pools that locked on to their target as he listened intently.

It took him about a month to ask her out, but they hit it off really well. It started out as a casual friendship, which didn't seem to cause any problems with her or Elina. In fact, Elina seemed to really enjoy it when Phillip came over. He played with her and taught her how to throw a softball. They wrestled and laughed, played checkers, and seemed to become regular pals, but one night when she saw them kiss each other, she ran off to pout. Darcy talked with her about it and she seemed to understand. When it seemed Elina had accepted their relationship, they got married, but shortly after Phillip moved in with them she started throwing tantrums whenever Phillip asked her to do anything, even simple things like pick up her clothes.

"You're not my daddy! I don't have to listen to you!" She would yell at him, and then close herself off in her room. Phillip tried everything. Being nice didn't seem to help, and being forceful definitely worsened the problem. Finally, Darcy suggested that he take her out to do things alone, trying to reestablish the bond they had seemed to have in the beginning. It was rocky at first, but the more time they spent together, the more things seemed to improve. Then Danny came along, and it appeared his birth had healed the rift. Darcy supposed having a brother made Elina feel that she was part of a family, instead of a kid caught between two grownups.

Now they functioned like a family, except for the fact that Elina never called Phillip, Daddy. Darcy knew it bothered him a little, but he didn't push the issue, allowing Elina her own space. Still, there were times like these, with Dan's death on her mind, when Darcy wondered just how things would be if Dan were still alive. No doubt they would not have had to go through the struggles they had endured, but they had learned much from their trials, and her relationship with her daughter was strong, much stronger than it would have been had Elina been sharing the attentions of both her father and her mother.

It was hard for Darcy to conjure up Dan's image from the depths of her mind these days. It was as if she had put him far away, and she struggled to get his features just right. One thing which hadn't faded from her memory was his smile. She had a constant reminder of that in Elina. Every once in a while, she would take down the picture of the two of them and stare at his face, trying to memorize it once again, so that when she reached into her mind, she would be able to retrieve it, but it was no use. Dan was a part of the past, and she knew she should keep him there, as much for herself as for Phillip.

Darcy turned over on her side, her back to Phillip. She felt his warmth next to her, in the spot that had been so cold for nearly seven years. He was a good man, kind and compassionate. He was handsome as well, and an excellent lover, tending to her needs and desires, sharing his own. It was a comforting feeling having his body against hers. She felt him stir, and his hand caressed her back. Then he reached around her a pulled her close. In his warm embrace, Darcy drifted off to sleep, her bed warm, her house once again a home, and her dreams filled with the sleepy, innocent visions of her children.

Six

The silence of the night was broken, first by the shrieks of a small little girl, and then by an infant, startled out of his sleep. Phillip rushed into Elina's room, while Darcy tried to hush little Danny. But Elina's screams of terror did not cease, and the baby could not be silenced as long as his world was in turmoil.

"Elina, sweetheart, please calm down. You're scaring Danny. What's wrong baby? Did you have a bad dream?"

Phillip tried to consol her, but it was as if she didn't even recognize his presence. He continued.

"Elina, please talk to me. What happened?"

No response but the screams. Phillip, desperate to fix the interruption to the night, decided to trade places with Darcy. He left Elina crying in her room and went to Darcy's side.

"Here, give Danny to me. See if you can calm her down. She won't even talk to me."

Darcy didn't even bother to question him. The same thing had happened the week before, and she knew Phillip had no power over the situation. She went to her daughter's side, and wrapped her arms around her. Rocking back and forth with the child in her arms, she whispered.

"Shhhhh. Hush now baby. Mommy is here."

At first, it had no effect, but as she whispered over and over the child began to quiet, and her screams turned to muffled snubs.

"Shhhhh. Tell mommy what happened. Quiet now Elina, tell mommy what happened."

Again and again she whispered.

"Hush baby, hush now. Tell mommy what's wrong."

Elina pressed her head into her mother's chest. Her tears left little wet spots on Darcy's gown. Her body shuddered with each breath. Her arms clung in a desperate hug to Darcy. Gradually, her breathing began to slow. When, at last, it seemed she had calmed enough to talk, Darcy held Elina's face between her hands and kissed hr forehead.

"Was it the same dream as before?"

Elina nodded.

"Tell me what happened."

Between snubs, Elina presented the images which had awakened the terror within.

"We were at the park."

"Just you and me, like before?" Darcy inquired.

"Uh huh. And there was this man standing under the tree. He was watching us play. Then he waved at us, and he was looking at me, like he wanted me to come closer. You told me it was okay and I should go over there. At first, I was scared, but when I got a little closer I could see that it was Daddy."

"So, the man was Daddy Dan, and he wanted you to come over to him?"

"Uh huh. And when I realized it was Daddy, I started running, because I wanted to talk to him, but he just kept moving away. I ran harder and harder, but he was still far away. And pretty soon I was so tired, and I couldn't run any more, but I kept walking and walking, and no matter how long I couldn't reach him. When I turned around to look for you, it was dark and I was alone."

"So, is that what scared you? Was it because it was dark?"

She shook her head.

"Mommy, it seemed like I was running forever, but I still couldn't get to Daddy."

Elina began to cry again, and Darcy pulled her close.

"I'm sorry sweetheart. But it's just a dream. Daddy is always with us, even though we can't see him, he is in our hearts."

"I just wanted him to hug me, but I couldn't get there."

"Elina, Daddy would hug you if he could, but he can't, not the way we are use to, anyway. He can only hug our hearts. But if you need a hug, you can always get one from me, and Phillip would hug you too, if you let him. We love you, Elina. You don't have to be scared, because we will always be here for you. You know that don't you?"

The little girl nodded.

"Are you okay now? Can you go back to sleep?"

"I'll try, but will you stay with me? Just 'til I go back to sleep."

"Okay."

Darcy tucked the covers in around her daughter. Lying down on the bed beside her, she snuggled close. In the dark, she stared at the ceiling, wondering just what it was that had brought about her daughter's nightmares. She had seemed to be comfortable with Dan's death, when she was younger. Something had started this, yet she had no idea what it might have been. She thought back on recent conversations, but found nothing she could pinpoint as the root of the problem.

When, at last, she heard the sounds of restful slumber from the little girl beside her, Darcy rose and tiptoed out of the room. She stopped by Danny's crib to check on him. Then she slipped into bed beside her husband.

Nestled in the warmth of Phillip's nearness, Darcy found her thoughts lost in the past. Dan moved back into her mind once again. She remembered the early parts of their relationship and how much fun they used to have. It was a carefree time, those days. Little trips to Padre Island, to Galveston Bay, and to the hill country near Austin; it was a time for just the two of them.

Darcy considered herself a fortunate person. She had been given the chance to love two wonderful men, each of them different in their own way. Dan was fun, pure and simple, while Phillip was somewhat more serious, his humor less obnoxious. Phillip accepted his commitment to the welfare of his family as his first priority. There was a deeper maturity to him, not that he was boring, or that he couldn't be playful. He could, but it was different. Dan was quick with the wit and light on his feet.

Having a family changes a person; responsibilities take on greater meaning, and the things which seemed so simple before become more complicated. Those little complications cause people to grow and change in ways they never before imagined. Adaptation becomes a necessity. It is through those adaptations that people mature, gaining a deeper dimension to their personalities.

A simple trip to the Gulf these days would be quite an ordeal. Loading the van, making sure there were enough diapers, keeping up with the children among strangers, things that add up to much more than simply hopping into the car and taking off. Still it would be fun. And it had been quite a long time since she had done anything like that. But could they afford it? She wasn't sure, but perhaps that's just what they needed, a chance to get away for a few days.

Darcy made up her mind to talk to Phillip about it in the morning. Then she turned to look at the clock. It was nearly three in the morning. She knew she must somehow turn her mind off and get to sleep, if she was to get up in time for work.

She nuzzled up against Phillip's back. He was warm and comforting, and as she slid her hand over his chest, she felt her body begin to relax. Phillip felt her through his grogginess; he felt her touch, and his hand reached up to brush against her arm. His warm touch sent a relaxing tingle through her body. Darcy closed her eyes, and drifted away to the sounds of the surf rolling in her mind.

The following morning, Darcy was surprised at Phillip's reaction to her suggestion.

"Sounds like a good idea. Think we can afford it?"

Darcy tried to hide her astonishment in her reply.

"Uh, I think we could squeeze it in. It wouldn't cost too much if we just went for a weekend. We could stay in League City; that would probably be cheaper than staying on the island."

"Well, I guess I could call around and check out some prices. I don't have too much going on this morning at the office. I'll see what I can come up with, and then we'll decide."

This was going better than she expected.

"Sure. Well, I'll talk to you about it this evening. I've got to get going. You have time to drop off the kids?"

"Yeah, I'll take care of it."

She kissed the kids goodbye and then she hugged her husband.

"Phillip, thanks. I love you."

"Love you too. Have a good day."

The weekend at the bay seemed just what the doctor ordered. In Kemah, they watched the boats entering and exiting the harbor from the deck of a small seafood place. Elina got a kick out of dropping bits of food to the fish down below. And they all enjoyed the beach on Galveston Island. It was just at the end of the heavy tourist season, so the crowds weren't much of a hassle.

While Phillip and the kids played in the sand at the water's edge, Darcy soaked up the warm rays of sunlight basking down upon the island. Every so often her motherly instincts caused her to peek down the beach at them. Danny looked so little against the vast expanse of water in the background. Elina, danced at the water's edge, jumping up in the air each time a wave rolled in to the shore. Darcy had been sure to coat them all down with sunscreen, but she cautioned Phillip just the same.

"Now, don't let him stay out in that sun too long. If he starts to get too warm, bring him back here and put him under the umbrella."

"Yes, ma'am." Phillip said submissively.

"Mommy can I get some seashells to take home?"

Elina had been carrying around a sand bucket she'd picked out at Wal-Mart since they'd packed the van.

"Sure, baby, but wash them off good. I don't want that sand all over my van."

Despite all of her cautions, when they got home, all were sunburned, and sand seemed to have pervaded everything. Still, the trip seemed to do them all good. Elina slept without any nightmares, the entire time they were gone.

Elina's relationship with Phillip seemed to have improved as well. They did everything together, building castles in the sand, chasing after sand crabs along the beach, picking out the best shells to take home. Elina especially enjoyed burying her stepfather in the sand.

As she had often done on her trips with Dan, Darcy documented everything on film. She even had a picture of the family taken when they went out for a boat ride, and that one she hoped to put upon her dresser at home, where the one of her and Dan had been. It was a great shot with smiles all around. Elina was seated in Phillip's lap, the wind blowing her golden locks of hair, and the blue-green of the bay in the background. It was a beautiful shot.

Looking at the images imposed upon the Kodak paper, it seemed their family had grown so much closer in just that one weekend. And in truth, they had gained immensely from the experience. Elina especially. She had even slipped and called Phillip "Daddy" once when they were out on the beach. Darcy knew he had been touched by the moment, but, wisely, he hadn't made a big thing out of it.

In the days that followed their trip, the Henning household grew to accept the idea that everything was finally settling down to normal.

Seven

"You'll never be my Daddy! You made my mommy hide my daddy's pictures! I hate you! I hate you! I hate you!"

The words echoed in his head, over and over. They ate at the core of him and caused him to think thoughts he never believed he was capable of thinking. She was just a child, but she could make the entire household miserable in a matter of moments. It wasn't the sweet little girl he had known before all this took place; he loved her. He loved her dearly, but when that little girl disappeared to be replaced by this angry, hateful little demon, a part of him regretted ever becoming entangled in her life.

He knew the angel and the demon were one and the same, however, and he could not have one without the other. He knew, deep down inside he knew, it was not he who she hated; it was the situation in which she found herself. And it was that knowledge, that confidence, on which he relied to keep his own feelings in check.

Phillip felt he was more observant than Darcy, and possibly slightly less connected. He had the advantage of watching from a distance, and he had concluded, from his observations, watching her and listening to her, that it was fear which drove his stepdaughter into her fits of madness. Elina feared, possibly the same way Darcy had once feared, if she ever acknowledged him as part of her life, she would somehow forget her real father. And although it was too much for her young mind to understand, he tried to get through to her. That's why he was so patient with her, that's why he made himself available to her, and that's why he kept his temper in check. But it hurt; it hurt more than he would ever admit.

Even with this knowledge, Phillip was nearly at his wits end. Darcy pleaded with him to stay vigilant, to be patient.

"She'll come around, Phillip. I know she will; it just takes time."

But it had been nearly a year since Danny was born and, although there were periods in which things seemed to improve, over time, her behavior had actually seemed to worsen. He knew it must be hard on her, never knowing her father. Phillip did his best to let her know he had no intention of taking Dan's place in her life, but Elina had built a wall he could not penetrate. They would get along fine for long periods of time, and then she would just snap.

This latest episode started because she found her father's pictures put away in the cedar chest in the closet. Why she had been digging in there was another story, but she had found them, and it was he who she blamed for having put them away. Darcy tried to explain the reasons behind her decision to put them away, but when she got like that, no one could get through to her. She had only one place in which she could focus her anger, and that was in his direction.

"I hate you. You want to take my daddy's place, but I won't let you. You're not my daddy. My daddy is good. He loves me."

"Elina, I don't want to take your daddy's place. Your daddy died, I know that hurts you, but it isn't my fault. I just want to make you, and your mommy, and Danny happy. Your daddy will always be your daddy. I know he loves you, and I love you too, sweetheart, but I can't have you always getting upset with me because your daddy is gone."

She stomped off to her room. He knew she would stay there for a while, and when she reemerged she would be a totally different child. It was almost as if she had something built up inside her she had to release, and then, once it was out, she was fine, at least for a while. They had considered counseling; they had even talked to the minister at their church about it, but Darcy had been reluctant and kept hoping things would eventually work out on their own. But in Philip's mind, that didn't seem possible.

"I'll go talk to her."

That was Darcy. She felt like anything could be fixed with a little loving conversation.

"It won't do any good, Darcy. Oh, she'll get over it for now, but then she'll explode again later. It'll be over some other little thing that makes her realize Dan isn't in her life anymore. She needs help. We need help. I can't go on like this. I love her, and I want to be part of her life, but something is causing her to keep me at a distance. She needs someone who can help her find out what is troubling her."

Darcy shook her head.

"Phillip, just give it some more time. She's been through a lot. She doesn't seem as bad to me. It's been quite a while since she got this upset."

"Darcy, when are you going to admit she needs help?"

"Please, Phillip, just a little more time. I'll talk to her. She'll do better. You'll see."

Phillip wasn't convinced, but he knew the conversation wasn't going anywhere.

"I'll try Darcy, but I don't know how much more of this I can take."

Darcy turned and walked down the hall toward Elina's room. She knocked on the door; opening it, she peeked inside.

"Can we talk?"

Elina was unresponsive. Her head was buried into her pillows. Darcy entered the room and sat on the edge of her bed.

"Elina, sweetheart, we need to talk. You shouldn't have yelled at Phillip like that. It wasn't his fault that daddy's pictures were in the chest. I put them there a long time ago, before we ever met Phillip."

Elina uncovered her face.

"Why mommy? Why did you hide daddy's pictures from me?"

"Baby, I didn't hide daddy's pictures from you. I hid them from myself. I was tired of feeling bad because daddy was gone. I was tired of blaming myself for the accident. I had to get past it. I know you don't understand, but we have to let go of daddy, and go on with our lives. He will always be part of us, but he isn't here anymore. He keeps trying to go to heaven, and we keep trying to pull him back, but he can't come back. No one can."

"Elina, maybe it would help if you thought of Phillip as the person daddy sent to look after us in his place. I know Phillip is not your real daddy, but he loves you, just like Daddy Dan did. Maybe Daddy Dan sent Phillip to take his place or maybe God did, but either way, he wants to love you and you just won't let him. Why Elina? Why won't you let Phillip love you?"

"Because he's not my daddy."

"But your daddy is dead. Don't you understand? He's not coming back. He won't ever come back. Phillip is here, and he wants to do the things your daddy would do if he were still here. He wants to love you, and play with you, and help you with your schoolwork. He wants to take you places and be with you. He wants to be the kind of daddy your real daddy never had a chance to be, but you won't let him."

Darcy looked into Elina's eyes, still wet with tears. There was a deep sadness in them, a sadness, which hid itself beyond the surface, buried deep within her blue-eyes. Then Elina startled her with her next question.

"Did I kill my daddy?"

Darcy was caught off guard. It seemed to come from out of the blue, and it gave her a chilling hint to the underlying problems her child faced.

"No, of course not! What would give you that idea?"

"Well, you said that daddy died because he was coming to see me."

"I said that daddy died *when* he was coming to see you, not because he was coming to see you. Daddy died in a car accident. It could have happened at any time, sweetheart. It just happened to take place when he was on his way to the hospital to see both of us. It wasn't your fault; you weren't even born yet. I use to think that maybe it was my fault because I asked him to hurry, but it wasn't my fault either. Sometimes those things just happen. Elina, you may be too young to understand this, but you can't blame yourself for daddy's death."

The young girl was silent for a few moments, contemplating her mother's words, her sad eyes revealing the confusion within. In a world surrounded by stuffed animals, baby dolls, and pink and white lace, Elina struggled to understand concepts with which many adults struggled.

Then, as if she had awakened on a new day, her face changed, as she gave Darcy one of those smiles that reminded her of Dan. She threw her little arms around her mother's neck, and offered her apology.

"I'm sorry mommy. I'll try to be nice."

Amazed at the change, Darcy hugged her back in acceptance.

"Well, it's not just me who you should apologize to; Phillip deserves to hear the same thing."

"I know. I'll go tell him. Please don't be mad at me mommy."

"Elina, I'm not mad at you, but I am disappointed in how you acted. Now, go talk to Phillip."

Elina slowly made her way to the living room, and stood looking down at the floor in front of Phillip.

"I'm sorry, Phillip. I shouldn't have acted so badly. Please don't be mad at me."

Phillip took her hand and led her to a seat on his knee.

"Elina, I'm not going to say that I wasn't mad, because I was, but if you think we can work this out, I'll try as well. I don't want you to think I am trying to take your daddy's place, but I do think you could make a place in your heart for me as well, if you just try."

Elina looked into the eyes of her stepfather. "I'll try."

But even as she promised him, Phillip held little hope their struggles were over. He felt they would never be over, until Elina came to grips with the demons which tortured her. He had seen them in her sleep. At night when she was asleep, he saw how fitfully she slept. It had been quite a while since they had been awakened in the night by her screams, but Phillip knew the nightmares still continued to haunt her. He could hear her mumble in her dreams, and he knew she was struggling with the fear which gripped her in the night. Until she was able to meet those nightmares head on, she would always struggle with the fact that her father had left this world at the same moment in which she had entered it.

Eight

The shrill sound of the phone ringing pierced the night. Darcy sat up with a start. Grabbing for the receiver she knocked over a glass of water.

"Crap."

She heard the water spilling off the surface of the night table and on to the carpet between the rings. Forcing herself to disregard the puddle in the carpet, she grabbed once again for the phone.

"Hello."

She could hear the grogginess in her own voice. She glanced over at the other side of the bed where Phillip continued to snore.

"Mrs. Henning?" The voice on the other end sounded irritated.

"Yes."

"You need to come over here and pick up your daughter."

"Who is this?"

"This is Connie Fuller."

"Elina is asleep."

"No, she's not. She's sitting in my living room. I caught her climbing in Jeffery's window."

"That can't be. She went to bed at ten o'clock."

"Mrs. Henning, your daughter is sitting in front of me now."

"Mrs. Fuller, can you hold on just a minute?"

"Gee, why not?" Mrs. Fuller's voice oozed with sarcasm.

"I'll just be a second."

"Oh, by all means, take your time."

Darcy laid the phone down and scampered down the hallway. She quietly eased the door open to Elina's room. Despite her neighbor's claim, as she scanned the darkened room, she was surprised to find the bed empty and the curtains waving in the breeze. She could feel the blood beginning to boil as she made her way back to her bedroom. Picking up the receiver she began to apologize to the woman on the other end of the line.

"Mrs. Fuller, I'm terribly sorry. I'll wake up Elina's stepfather and one us will be right over."

She nudged Phillip as she placed the phone back on the hook.

"Phillip, wake up."

He stirred.

"Phillip!" She said more forcefully.

Phillip's eyes popped open.

"What?"

"You have to go over to the Fuller's house."

Phillip rubbed his eyes and glanced at the clock on the table beside the bed.

"It's two o'clock in the morning."

"I know what time it is. I just got off the phone with Connie Fuller. She caught Elina sneaking in Jeffery's window."

"What? I thought she was in bed."

"So did I."

Phillip threw back the covers from the bed and swung his feet to the floor.

"I checked her room. She's not there and the window was open."

"That girl…" Phillip cut himself off.

"Just go get her, okay?"

His frustration grew as he dressed. By the time he was closing the front door behind him, he was nearly ready to explode. The Fullers lived three blocks away. Jeffery was in Elina's eighth grade class. The two of them hung out together after school pretty often. He was a nerdy looking kid with thick glasses. He'd always seemed rather harmless, not exactly the kind of Romeo who would cause a girl to slip off in the middle of the night. As the headlights pierced through the darkness of the night, Phillip mumbled his aggravation.

"What in the world got into her? What's a girl her age think she's doing sneaking around that time of the morning anyway?"

He pulled up in front of the Fuller's house noticing theirs was the only house on the block with the lights on. The sound of the car door closing behind him seemed out of place in the quiet night. As did the sound of the doorbell as he pushed the button.

Connie Fuller answered the door in a well-worn peach colored house robe. Even though she stood nearly a foot below him, her disheveled blonde hair and the disturbed look on her face sent an intimidating message. Under other circumstances she might have been an attractive woman, but at the moment she looked like she'd stepped out of a horror movie. He noted, the only thing missing to complete her wardrobe was a meat cleaver. She nearly pushed Elina out the door as she opened it.

"Mr. Henning, I'd appreciate it if you would make sure this doesn't happen again. If I hadn't heard Jeffery's window opening, who knows what might have happened. It is a poor state of affairs when a young girl like her is out wandering the neighborhood this time of night."

"I can assure you we had no idea she had snuck out of the house. I will address this with Elina and make sure it doesn't happen again."

"It's girls like her that get good boys into trouble." She emphasized her words by pointing her index finger at Elina.

"Hold on just a minute. I will admit I am disappointed in Elina's actions, but if your son hadn't wanted her to enter his room, he wouldn't have opened the window or invited her over."

"Jeffery is a good boy. He wouldn't have done anything like this if he wasn't being tempted by this…this seductress."

"Seductress? I'd hardly call this a situation for that kind of statement. They're in the eighth grade. Mrs. Fuller, Elina has been over here numerous times, just as Jeffery has been to our home, and there has never been any trouble between them; certainly nothing which would warrant this kind of name calling."

"What else do you call a girl who sneaks into a boy's bedroom in the middle of the night? She's a home wrecker."

"Okay, we're done here. I'm not going to stand here and take your verbal abuse of my stepdaughter. She may have made a mistake, but she wasn't the only one involved. Elina, come with me."

He took Elina by the shoulder and turned her toward the car.

"Goodnight, Mrs. Fuller." He said as he walked away.

When they were in the car, Elina spoke up.

"Thanks for taking up for me." She said somberly.

"You're not off the hook just because she's in denial about the role her son played in this."

"I didn't figure I was."

"What were you thinking? Why in the world would you be sneaking out at two in the morning?"

"Would you have preferred I snuck out at ten thirty?"

"Don't get smart."

"Look, we weren't going to do anything. I was messaging Jeff on the computer. He was awake and I was awake. He asked if I wanted to come over and talk instead of messaging. I figured I could get back home before you noticed I was gone. You were snoring loud enough to shake the house."

"Aside from the fact that girls your age don't need to be out at that time of the morning, you don't need to be at a boy's house without permission. I just don't understand what makes you think you have the freedom to just slip out whenever you want."

"It's no big deal, Phillip. We were just going to talk."

"It is a big deal, Elina. You can't just come and go as you please."

"But I was awake any way. What's it matter if I'm awake here or at Jeff's house? I've been there plenty of times during the day."

"Don't try to excuse your way out of this. You have no right to take off without permission and you have no business being out at two in the morning. You are in the eighth grade. How far are you planning to go when you're in high school?"

"I don't see why you have to make such a stink over this. We were just talking."

"Oh, and you thought his parents would have no problem with you sneaking in his room in the middle of the night. If it wasn't such a big deal, why didn't you just ring the doorbell and go through the front? Why'd you think it was necessary to sneak through his window?"

"I didn't want to wake them up."

Phillip could see he wasn't getting anywhere. In the morning he would seal the window shut. Obviously she couldn't be trusted and they couldn't take a chance on her sneaking around again in the future. Aside from the trouble she could get into in a boy's room in the middle of the night, there's no telling what could happen to her when she was out wandering alone.

The lights of the car reflected off the garage door as he pulled in the drive.

"Look, just go to your room. We'll talk about this in the morning. I'm tired."

"Fine."

She slammed the car door as she exited. Before he reached the house, he heard her slam the front door as well.

When he entered the house, Darcy met him at the door.

"What happened?"

"I picked her up at the house. I had to listen to that Fuller woman's verbal abuse. I tried to talk to her on the way home and couldn't get anywhere. She can't see that she did anything wrong."

"I'll talk to her."

"Sure." He said. "I'm going to bed."

"What are we going to do to keep her from sneaking out in the future?"

"I'll take care of that in the morning."

As Phillip undressed, he could hear her sharing her story with her mother.

"Mom, it's no big deal!"

He was growing so weary of the constant battle. He'd been dealing with it so long. At first it was just the moodiness and the nightmares. As she grew older it was becoming more about the rebellion. She fought against them at nearly every step. He couldn't imagine what it would be like when she entered high school. The trouble she could cause for them was unimaginable. Besides her parents, there was her brother to think about. How was her rebellious example going to impact Danny?

So far she'd just pushed the boundaries of their resolve; staying up late, arguing against their rules and questioning their decisions. Thirty minutes late for curfew, not coming straight home from school, telling them their rules were stupid; she was testing them to see if they would bend and trying to see how far she could go before they put a stop to her antics. Darcy couldn't see it, but he knew they were brewing up for a real battle.

The girl just seemed to be constantly running from something. He knew it was some kind of fear which was driving her, but he couldn't place his finger on it. There were times when they got along just fine, then when it seemed things were falling in place, she'd ratchet it up a notch. It was almost as if she couldn't allow herself to be content or normal.

Phillip moved back into bed. He knew it would be a while before Darcy would come back and settle down. He needed sleep. Work was going to come early. Of course, as tired as he was, it was going to take his body some time to settle down from being so keyed up. He hated nights like this. He'd find himself staring at the clock counting down the hours and minutes he had left before the alarm went off, which would in turn add to the frustrations keeping him awake in the first place.

He was still awake when Darcy came back and slipped into bed in the dark. He didn't turn to face her or try to give her any indication he was awake. She'd just want to talk about Elina and it would end up keeping him awake even longer. His charade worked, because his eventual sleep came as he played possum.

It seemed like no time at all had passed when the alarm went off and he stared at it trying to find a way to squeeze out a few more minutes of sleep. When he had played with time as long as he dared, he lifted up out of bed his head aching from the lack of sleep. It was going to be a long day and it was a good thing both Darcy and Elina were able to sleep in. He knew he was going to be as grumpy as a bear awakened during hibernation.

Nine

As time passes the unusual begins to seem quite normal. As senses dull to overexposure, and acceptance seems to be the only way to handle a situation. Over time, and the relentless pleas of his wife, Phillip Henning grew to allow, even expect Elina's behavior to remain unchanged. It became normal to tiptoe around her feelings, striving to keep the fire from igniting. Even Danny grew up to accept his sister's rather predictable unpredictability.

The reflection of red lights flashing in the driveway, a parent's nightmare, flickered against the living room curtains. Phillip answered the door. He had expected this to occur, even as he hoped it wouldn't. Elina's rebelliousness was clear, and it was simply a matter of time before it led her to this point.

Greeting him as he opened the door, the police officer's disposition was serious, but polite.

"Mr. Pearson?"

"No, my name is Henning, Phillip Henning. Elina's father passed away when she was younger. I'm her stepfather."

He hated having to explain that to everyone. Why Darcy hadn't consented to allow him to adopt Elina years ago, escaped him. He had raised the child. She should have had his name, but it was too late now. Elina would never consent now. There were times when his stepdaughter acted as though she detested the sight of him, she'd never have his name.

Though there were moments when their relationship could appear to be on the growing path, her teen years seemed to push those moments further and further apart. Although, her mother continued to hold out some hope she would somehow come to her senses, he did not. He had come to believe that his stepdaughter would never realize she was her own enemy in her quest for happiness, and independence. They would never live in peace until Elina could learn to deal with her issues. With the police officer standing in front of him, it seemed they were far from making that happen.

"Well, sir, I'm going to have to ask you to come down to the station with me. Your daughter, uh, excuse me, stepdaughter, was caught driving under the influence. It seems she ran a red light, and nearly hit two other motorists in the process."

Darcy had stepped into the doorway just in time to hear the officer's account.

"Was anyone hurt?" She asked.

"No ma'am. Fortunately, not, however the car has been impounded, and you're daughter's license will probably be suspended. That's up to the district attorney."

Phillip turned from the door. "I'll get my coat."

"Phillip, I want to go with you." Darcy insisted.

"No, you stay here with Danny. I'll take care of her." The aggravation in his voice couldn't be hidden.

"You'll need your id, sir." The officer told him. "We'll release her into your custody, since she is a minor."

As Phillip kissed his wife goodbye, she whispered in his ear. "Don't be too hard on her, until you find out all of the facts."

When he saw his stepdaughter, Phillip felt the blood rush to his head, the anger seething just below the surface. Elina was not merely under the influence; she was drunk. And, as usual, she displayed no remorse or even responsibility for her actions.

"It's a wonder you didn't get someone killed, including yourself." Phillip chastised on the way home.

"Oh, come on, Phillip. Loosen up."

"Don't tell me to loosen up young lady. You've probably gotten your license suspended, and you've gotten my car impounded. You'll be lucky if they don't send you away to some juvenile facility."

"You wish! You'd like that wouldn't you! You never have liked me. I'd be out of your hair, if they sent me away."

Her voice was slurred as she spoke, and the smell of alcohol emitted into the air with each word.

"Don't you talk like that, and don't raise your voice to me. That's not true and you know it. It's you, Elina. You are the one with the problem and you can't even see it."

He paused in thought, and when he spoke again his voice had softened.

"Elina, you are your own worst enemy. You seem hell bent for self-destruction. Why?"

She scoffed at him. "Whatever."

"Elina, you can't go on treating the rest of the world as if it doesn't matter. I don't know what I've got to do to get through to you. I don't know why you hate me so much that you won't even hear a word I say. All I've every tried to do is be a good stepfather, yet you treat me like I'm your worst enemy. I'm not your enemy. I'm on your side."

"It didn't look like you were on my side back at the police station. You wanted to kill me. Admit it. You were so mad you were ready to explode."

"Okay, I was mad. I had a right to be mad. But that doesn't mean I'm not on your side. I can support you as a person, and still dislike your actions. I am on you side, but you broke the law. You deserve whatever punishment they offer you. The law is there to keep you alive."

"Whatever! I knew you'd take their side. You hate me!"

There was no reasoning with her at this point. Phillip knew that, and he could only hope her mother would be able to make more sense to her. They were silent the rest of the way home; he out of some fear of escalating the situation, and she out of some disturbed, self-induced indignation.

Her mother, as Phillip expected, treated her as though she had been wronged.

"Oh, my baby. Look what's happened to you. You look terrible. Why don't you go clean up for bed? We can talk about this in the morning. You need to get some rest now."

Elina sulked off.

"Darcy, you don't have to act like it's not her fault. She's the one that broke the law." Phillip admonished.

"Phillip, treating her like a criminal won't help the matter. She's obviously tired, there isn't any sense interrogating her tonight."

"She isn't obviously tired, she's obviously drunk. And that is her fault. She made the decision to drink. And her decision to drive while drunk could have gotten her, or her friends, or some innocent bystander killed. She needs to know that behavior isn't acceptable in this house."

Darcy could sense his frustration and she knew he was right, but it didn't seem to make any sense to try to hash it out when she wouldn't even remember what they had discussed in the morning.

"I know she's at fault, but we're not going to get through to her tonight." She argued. "We'll let her sleep it off and discuss it in the morning."

"Darcy, we won't have anymore success in the morning than we'll have tonight. I've told you before the girl needs professional help. It is beyond our ability to fix."

"She doesn't need help. She needs parents that understand what she is going through."

Phillip shook his head and walked away. He was tired of discussing it. It always went the same way. Darcy just couldn't see past a certain point. It was almost as if she was admitting some kind of failure on her part if Elina needed help outside the family. There was no sense in arguing, they had done enough of that thru the years.

The next morning the conversation went as he expected. Elina apologized, saying it wouldn't happen again. She knew her mother, and she knew that was what she wanted to hear, so she said it, and then put it behind her.

The following Friday, she was out all night long, running around with boys they didn't know, hanging out with girls of questionable reputations. It was as if the scare of going to jail or juvenile detention had no impact upon her whatsoever. Her parents, try as they might, seemed to have no control over her. They grounded her, took away her privileges, and forbid reckless friendships, yet all they gained was bitterness and contempt.

The cycle continued on for the next two years. She barely passed a course in school, and as far as Phillip was concerned, it would be a miracle if she even graduated from high school. She displayed a total disregard for responsibility, commitment, and authority. She was impulsive and undisciplined. And her parents, even the brother she had doted over as a young girl, were merely passing acquaintances, people she knew, certainly not anyone she cared about.

Then came the bombshell. She delivered it just after the beginning of her senior year.

"I'm thinking about dropping out of school and getting a job."

Her parents looked up at her from their plates with astonishment. Darcy was the first to reply.

"Why on earth would you consider doing something like that? She asked.

"I just think I should start thinking about moving out on my own. I'm tired of school anyway. I don't plan on going to college, so what difference does it make?"

Phillip couldn't refrain. "I'll tell you what difference it makes. First of all, you aren't going to get any kind of a decent job, without an education. Secondly, you aren't old enough to make that kind of decision. And thirdly, as long as you are under my roof, you'll continue to go to school."

"Well, that's just it. Maybe I don't want to be under your roof anymore, Phillip. Maybe I'm tired of hearing about your rules. You, you, you…Phillip, all you think about is you! What about what I want? When will you two give a damn about what I want?"

"Watch your mouth young lady. You don't need to talk like that. We are your parents, and we'll decide what is best for you." Phillip had taken this long enough.

"You mean mom is my parent. You're just my stepfather." Elina snapped back.

"You're right Elina. I'm just your stepfather, the guy you won't let into your life. You don't want me to care about you; you don't want me involved in your life; and you don't want to live under my roof. Why is that Elina? What have I ever done to you to cause you to loath me as much as you do? Do you think I was responsible for your father's death, is that it? That's all I've ever been able to conclude, because I've never done anything else to cause you such grief. I've tried to always treat you as if you were my own. I've always made myself available to you when you needed me. So, tell me, tell the whole family, just why it is that you can't stand Phillip Henning."

Elina exploded from her chair, sending the dishes across the table. The entire episode was played out in front of her younger brother. She grabbed her coat and headed for the door.

"Just where do you think you are going, young lady."

She ignored Phillip's question, offering only her back as a response. Then she slammed the door on the way out.

"Why does she act like that?" Danny asked.

Darcy shook her head. "I don't know."

Somewhere in the night, she had slipped in, gathered her things, and slipped out without a word or a sound.

The officer had asked nearly every question imaginable. Though she had once thought her emotions couldn't possibly reach any closer to despair, after the nearly endless questioning Darcy felt worn to a frazzle. Her body felt like it was sinking into the surface of the couch.

Phillip sat beside her. He had remained patient and calm throughout, providing her with enormous stability in an incredibly tumultuous period of time.

Officer O'Reilly sat across from them on the other side of the coffee table. When he at last felt he had as much information as he needed, along with current pictures of Elina, O'Reilly stood to leave.

"Well, I think I have as much as we can use at this point. If you think of anything which might give us any further lead as to where she may have headed, just give us a call. We'll put out a bulletin to the surrounding area. Please understand, when it comes to runaways, our resources are sometimes limited."

Phillip stood and followed him to the door.

"Thank you, Officer."

When the police office had gone and they were alone with only each other to comfort, Darcy fell into Phillip's arms.

"I'll never forgive myself if something bad happens to her." Darcy mumbled.

"We'll find her. Who knows, she may even come to her senses and come home on her own." Phillip encouraged.

"But what if we don't?"

He kissed her head, while caressing her shoulders with his palms.

"We can't think that way. We have to keep hope."

"We don't know where she is, who she's with, or what she's doing. We don't even know if she's alive." Darcy argued.

"She hasn't been gone that long. She could be with a friend. We just have to be patient and keep looking."

Darcy wiped at her eyes. In all the commotion over her daughter, she'd lost track of Danny. She was suddenly startled.

"Where's Danny?"

Phillip smiled.

"It's okay. He's in his room. I just checked on him a few minutes ago."

"How's he taking this?"

"He's worried, but he's taking it better than us."

"I've got to go check on him." She said as she pulled away.

When she opened the door to Danny's room, she found him at his computer. He turned when he heard the door.

"Hey." Darcy offered

"Hey." Danny said as he turned back to his computer.

"How's it going?"

"Okay, I guess. Did she call?"

Darcy shook her head.

"Think she will?"

Darcy sat on the edge of his bed.

"I don't know. I guess we'll just have to wait and see. Any idea where she went?"

Danny scrunched the corner of his mouth and shook his head.

"She didn't say anything to you before she left?"

"No. She's been pretty quiet lately."

He sat silently for a few minutes.

"Mom?"

"Yes, Honey."

"Why's she so angry guys all the time?"

Darcy thought for a second.

"I really don't know, Baby. She just seems to carry it around with her. It doesn't come out all the time, but when it does, it comes full force. She doesn't seem to vent any of it toward you, does she?"

"No, we get along fine. She's pretty nice to me and even my friends. They all think she's cool."

Darcy smiled.

"They do? That's interesting. Has she ever said anything to you about what makes her that way?"

"No, not really. She talks about her dad sometimes and how she thinks it's her fault he died."

"She said that?"

"Well, not in those words, but I could tell what she meant."

Darcy couldn't hide the concerned look on her face.

"It wasn't her fault you know."

"I know. It was just an accident."

"Why doesn't she see that?" Darcy questioned out loud.

"I don't know, mom."

It had been nearly four days. The police had been notified, her friends had been called, and yet, they had no idea where she might have gone. No one had seen her. Each evening Darcy spent driving around looking, hoping to find someone who might have seen her daughter. She had become a tortured wreck. Her nerves were frazzled, and her body tired from lack of sleep. Her nights spent, sitting up, waiting… waiting… waiting… for just a word, for just a phone call, for some news, of her whereabouts, of her wanderings, of her reckless behavior, or …quite possibly, of her death.

The Rose Bares Its Blemish

Ten

Waves rolled against the smooth sandy beach. With each step her toes sunk into the cool morning sand. As she walked along with her sandals dangling between her fingers, she watched the sand squish up between her toes. Seashells dotted the shore ahead of her. Their images sometimes cleared, sometimes buried by the movement of the sand floating back and forth with each swell and fall of the water licking the beach. She saw herself somewhere in their example. She knew she was as much of the problem as anyone else. She'd float along feeling free and beautiful, then she'd be swallowed up by something bigger than her. As much as she struggled to stay on top, the grains of sand filtered over her and she fell beneath the surface; still there, but not quite visible.

She glanced up to watch the surface of the bay. Out in the distance a tanker made its way toward the ocean. It would leave the relative safety of the bay and move thru the gulf on out into the big wide ocean. Once there, it was alone to face whatever the world had to throw at it. Winds would come and whip up the waves; they'd crash against it, they'd lift and drop, they'd sway it, and if it could withstand the forces it would make its destination.

The breeze coming off the bay blew her hair into strands which danced at its direction. She spun on her heels to look back at her footprints in the sand. Those nearest her were still deep and the salt water pooled to fill the imprints; further down the beach she watched her presence disappear as the waves pulled and pushed; wiping out any sign she had ever been there.

Galveston hadn't quite recovered. Though the natural part of it appeared much as it had when she was a girl, the human part of it still struggled with return. Buildings along the seawall were in various states from destruction to construction to completion. This was a part of her happiest memories and it was a natural reaction to come here when she decided to leave. She hitched the whole way. She knew it was risky, being alone as she was, but then again, what did she have to lose?

She had no idea about her next move. She'd only been driven by two factors – the need to get away and the need get back; back to something which had given her some sense of normalcy. She didn't have a lot of money, so she'd have to make it last as long as she could. Other than what she'd stuffed in the backpack, she didn't have any other baggage than the baggage she carried inside. She'd spend at least a couple of nights on the beach, and then she'd make up her mind about what she was going to do next.

She watched the gulls dive at the sand picking up fragments of whatever had washed ashore. They continued as she walked along, giving little regard to her other than their noisy chatter. It was early spring and the beach was still nearly deserted. Earlier she had passed a jogger; his head beneath the hood of his sweater, the wire of his headphones snaking up his chest, his pace steady; he'd offered her less consideration than the birds.

Moving further up from the water into the dry sand, she made her way toward a clump of saw grass. She plopped down into the loose sand and crossed her legs. Her fingers played with the sand, scooping it up and letting it sift through between them. The gulls continue to swoop in their circular pattern, diving at the beach and lifting back up into the sky. She sat there watching and contemplating until she could no longer ignore the rumble in her stomach.

She pulled the pack from her shoulder and reached in feeling for the smooth surface of the apple. Then she zipped it up and threw it on the ground behind her back. She lay back on the sand using the pack as a pillow and stared up into the baby blue sky. She ate the apple while watching the white cottony puffs float above her. The sounds of the surf, the gulls, the breeze, and the gentle rub of the saw grass filled in the background music for the picture above her, allowing her mind to empty of all thought. For just a brief moment, everything was perfect in her life, and she let it stay that way until she'd finished her meal and for a few lazy minutes longer; long enough to slip gently off to sleep under its magical spell.

The sun had risen near its midday place when she finally stirred. She basked in its warm rays for just a few moments longer, feeling the heat against her face, seeing the red-orange glow through her eyelids. When she opened her eyes the day was older, the richness of the sky washed out to a pale blue. She looked out on the bay, her eyes squinting against the bright reflections. The tanker was gone, fearlessly moving on to the open ocean.

She lazily hung around the beach the rest of the day; only venturing away long enough to grab a hotdog and a Coke from a stand along the seawall. As evening began to fall she wandered further down the beach, gathering pieces of driftwood as she went. The sun was an orange sliver when she settled into the sand and dug a shallow hole. Using dried pieces of grass for tender, she struck a match and watched the flames as they began to grow.

When she was sure the fire had taken control over the dried flesh of the wood, she once again opened her pack and pulled the bag of marshmallows from within. She chuckled to herself as she realized her use of the pack for a pillow had caused the white puffs to clump together. Still she was able to rescue enough to slide onto a stick and dangle over the fire. She watched as they charred and blew out the orange glow before sticking the gooey treat into her mouth.

Again, pleasant memories surfaced and she found herself clinging to them as tightly as she could. She remembered the time they had spent the evening on the beach. It was such an adventure. The next day Phillip had driven them over to take the ferry. It was the first time she'd ever seen a dolphin. She'd been enamored with them for months afterward. She had pictures of dolphins on her wall and wore a glass dolphin pendant. Her mother bought her a backpack for school with glitter coated dolphins on it.

After she finished her snack, she settled back in the sand. Through sleepy eyes she watched the dance of the flames as they slowly hypnotized her into a deep restful sleep. The last conscious thoughts she had before she fell away were of her family back home. Somewhere in her dreams her father came to her once again. As a bystander, she saw the man under the tree and the little girl with the blond curls. He waved at her and she let go of her mother's hand to wave back. Then she started moving toward him, slowly at first, gradually picking up her pace until at last she ran to him as fast as her little legs could carry her. But try as she might, the man never grew closer. It was almost as if the girl was running on an escalator and each step carried her back to where she had begun.

Elina woke in a sweat. The cool breeze blew off the bay and the fire had settled down to coals. She sat up, getting her bearings. She could hear the roll of the waves nearby and as her eyes adjusted she saw the glow of the moon out upon the bay. She reached for another piece of driftwood, stirred the embers with the end of the branch, and added the wood. Orange tongues licked up into the black sky and she once again placed her head upon the pack to watch the wood as it slowly withered away under a force it could not control.

Giggles and laughter broke through the fog of sleep. It was Saturday on the Island and already there were families starting to gather. As they staked out their boundaries for the day, large umbrellas began to pop up on the beach. Heavy coolers filled with drinks and snacks were already being lugged into place. Blankets spread upon the sand like the squares on a chess board. Soon the open expanses of sand would be filled with people; their sounds would be a mingled blend of excitement and relaxation.

Her stomach growled, encouraging her to take a walk along the road lining the seawall to find something to eat.

She noticed the patrol car as it passed the second time. Sliding off into a stand of grass, she watched as the officer exited the car and stepped down off the seawall. He approached the jogger coming from the other end of the island. As they looked at something in his hands, the jogger turned and pointed back behind him. Apparently, he had taken more notice of her yesterday than she had first assumed.

It was time to go. She hated to leave the island; it was much sooner than she had planned, but Galveston was too small. She knew it was just a matter of time. They would find her and she would be forced back into a life where she just didn't fit. No, she wasn't going to let that happen. She wasn't going to give up her freedom that easily. She'd head back into the city and then she'd disappear for good.

Eleven

She'd emptied her savings account before she left Dallas. She'd spent nearly nothing while lingering along the beach at Galveston for the first week. Other than treating herself to a meal at the seafood restaurant in Kemah, the one they'd visited as a family when she was younger, she'd consisted on fruit and water, and marshmallows, of course.

The trip back into Houston had cost her no more than the trip down to Galveston since she'd used her thumb both ways. Although it pained her to leave the coastline, she knew she'd be able to hide out on the streets of Houston much better. Galveston just wasn't big enough. Perhaps, if she could stay hidden long enough for them to quit looking, she could make her way down to Corpus or even Mexico. If she planned her trip right, she could mingle in with the Spring Break crowds. That would be incredible. She could party like a rock star for days on end and then set out on her new life in earnest.

For now she had to play her cards carefully. She wasn't stupid; she knew she had to make what little money she had last. She'd spend a few days camping out on the streets or in a park. After all, it worked for homeless people, why not for her. Word on the street was that the place to hangout was around Hermann Park. There were shelters nearby to find refuge if things got out of hand.

She'd spread her money to different places, some in her shoe, some in the pockets of her blue jeans, and some in her backpack. If someone tried to rob her or take her bag, they wouldn't get it all.

The first night in Hermann Park was kind of unnerving. She'd been bothered by others throughout the night. It didn't take her long to realize she'd be better off between the buildings. At least she could find some place in which she could isolate herself from the others or some barrier which she could use to hide behind. Perhaps she could even stake out her territory like they did.

She made her way further into the streets, enjoying the continued warmth of the spring weather. As she wandered along in her sandals, she looked more like a young girl on a vacation than one of the homeless with whom she so desired to blend. She'd only brought a few pieces of clothing with her, her tennis shoes, a sweater (in the event the weather changed), some underwear, another top and pair of jeans. It would be enough to get by for a little while, and a little while was all she expected to spend down here among these unburdened wayfarers.

As the sun went down on her second night in Houston, she was still wondering the streets looking for a place to call home for the night. It hadn't been as easy as she had thought. Some of those people were incredibly territorial. More than once she had been faced with vicious confrontations when she'd tried to claim a corner by a dumpster or an awning in front of an office building.

Tired of walking she stumbled toward a dead end corner between two buildings. She was just preparing to settle down for the night, when a black man in a wheelchair rolled toward her.

"Get your white but out of my bedroom!" He shouted waving his arms at her hysterically.

She froze. She'd thought she'd seen all kinds down here on the street. She never expected to see a man in a wheelchair, let alone one who was prepared to fight for a space between two brick buildings.

"I was just looking for a place to rest."

"Well, keep looking girl. This is my turf, my place! I've lived here two years and ain't no prissy missy gonna squirm in here and take it away!"

"Can I sleep over there?" She asked pointing toward a doorway at the entrance of the partial alley.

"In my living room? Hell no!"

"Could I just be your guest for the night? I'll move on in the morning." She pleaded.

The man's demeanor seemed to change. Whether it was the respect she was showing for his territory or simply some moment of compassion, she wasn't sure, but he paused in thought and she was sure he was considering.

"Just for the night?"

"I promise. I'll even leave early if you want. I just need to rest a while."

His head cocked to the side.

"Can you pay?"

She reached for the pack on her back.

"I don't have much, what do you want?"

"Well, it's been a little while since supper at the shelter. You got anything I could snack on?"

"I've got an apple or some marshmallows."

He smiled a big toothless smile.

"Well, as you can see, that apple ain't gonna do me no good, but them marshmallows sounds pretty good."

She handed him the bag. Most were still clumped together. The fact that she'd used the pack as a pillow more than a time or two hadn't helped. Regardless the man seemed satisfied with his rent arrangement.

He stuck out his hand.

"I'm Willie Wheels." He said.

"I'm Allie." She lied.

He motioned to a spot beside him.

"Sit down there and let's chat a spell before you retire to the living room."

She slid down the wall to sit upon the ground beside him while Willie stuffed a marshmallow into his mouth and proceeded to gum it down.

"How long you been on the streets girl?" He said with his mouth full.

"Not long." She mumbled.

He licked his long, boney fingers.

"Willie Wheels don't go sticking his nose in other folks bidness, so I ain't a gonna ask you why you down here. But, my advice to you is you'd be best to go back home."

"I can't." She lied again.

"Well, in keeping with my strict, non-nosey policy, I ain't gonna ask you why, but you sure 'bout that?"

"My folks don't want me at home. I cause them too many problems."

"Is that your folks talkin' or you?"

"They've made it clear enough."

"I been out here on the streets a mighty long time. 'Seen all kinds. Lots of kids out here thinking they ain't wanted at home, but most times they is. They just chillins'. They don't know. They don't know how hard it is out here. The streets will wear you down. Make you do things you wouldn't do. You listenin' to me girl?"

She nodded.

"You ain't gonna make it long on apples and marshmallows. You been to a shelter?"

"No." She answered.

"You get yourself down to that shelter. They got a cot there you can sleep on. It beats the hell out of Willie's living room."

"Why aren't you there?"

"Well, I'm gonna ignore the fact that you breakin' my non-nosey policy and tell you. Willie don't need no shelter cuz Willie don't need nuthin'. I goes down there for a meal, but I ain't gonna sleep there. I got me this fine house here." He said motioning with his arms around the alley.

They talked on for a while, before Willie indicated he was done.

"Okay, now Willie's had his snack. You go off there to the living room and get to sleep."

Elina stood and started for the doorway. She stopped and turned around as Willie was moving his chair toward a black trash bag at the back of the alley.

"Mr. Willie?"

"What you want girl?" He asked, not sounding quite as annoyed as his words might otherwise indicate.

"Thanks."

"You just be on your way in the mornin'." He answered with his toothless smile.

Elina's night in the alley, though not what she would consider comfortable, was more restful than her night in the park. She wasn't sure if it was Willie's presence or the lack of others to disturb her.

True to her word, she was up and off down the street early the next morning. She didn't even bother to check with Willie. It was time to explore her options. She'd start by checking out the shelter Willie told her about.

Twelve

A glowing, white ball struggled to pierce the hazy, gray of the morning sky, a mixture of smog and dreariness offering its characteristic color to the world around her. She'd wandered drearily from Hermann Park up the streets toward her destination, wishing for the spring like weather to return. A light drizzle had begun but an hour before, yet it seemed to have gone on for an eternity. There was a chill to the air, which sent a shiver across her shoulders and down her spine. Her golden tresses were darkened with the moisture from the air and clung to her face, dripping icy droplets down her neck, sliding along the crevasse between her breasts. The chilling effects were far from erotic, far from ecstasy, and very near to eroding any remaining enthusiasm toward being on her own.

As she walked the streets, there was no pleasure absorbed from the solitude, no solace in the view of her surroundings, and no comfort in her condition. She had been walking for hours, mindlessly driven forward; occupying herself to pass the time, waiting as it ticked slowly along. After a restless night of sleeping under the cover of an awning, which hung out from the front of a pawn shop, being awakened by the goings on of the late night crowd, the change in the weather, and a couple of junkies looking for a quick thrill, she rose, regretfully resigned to begin the day with the meager portion of rest she had managed to scrape together. This had become her routine, her refuge from the monotony of a traditional, archetypical life.

She had celebrated her eighteenth birthday just the evening before, with a partial bottle of Smirnoff taken from a sleeping vagrant. He'd not stirred when she lifted the bottle from his rigid fingers, his head leaning heavily upon the brick wall behind him. She had taken the great caution to wipe off the rim of the bottle with her sweater. The vodka was cold against her lips, but as it moved down her throat, it left a warm trail burning on down toward her empty stomach. When the vodka hit the hollow cavity of her stomach she nearly wretched as the alcohol met with her sensitive interior. She held it down, however, stubbornly refusing to let go of her celebratory offering.

This is what she had become, and she would rather die than admit it was anything less than that for which she had hoped. She was on her own, independent of anyone to tell her how to live or what to do. She wanted to believe she was carefree and on the surface, where it counts from moment to moment, she was, but down deep, in that place she would never acknowledge to even exist, she was far from carefree. She was burdened beyond understanding; unsure of how she would survive; how she would eat or defend herself from the next male, or female for that matter, who tried to force their desires upon her; or if there would come a point at which she would even bother to defend herself anymore. Out on the streets, it was an every day, every night, occurrence, and she knew there was a possibility she would eventually grow weary of the struggle.

This was not the life of adventure she had hoped for when she left home, but she had to go on. There was a small voice inside of her which teased her into imagining what things were like at home. It wanted her to ponder upon her family and their happenings. It coaxed her into considering what her mother was doing. It urged her to consider whether or not Danny was getting along without her. It chided her into accepting the possibility that even Phillip might be missing her at the moment.

Each time the voice rose above a whisper into her consciousness, Elina would squelch it. She could not, would not, allow it to exist. To allow even the slightest consideration of any of these thoughts, would be detrimental to her freedom; for that would be an admission, an acknowledgement, of her failure and her weakness. Admitting failure in her struggle for independence would insure its demise, and her only weakness, the inability to be loved, was yet to reach her consciousness.

And so, Elina trudged on, seemingly oblivious to the cold around her and the frigidness of her heart, towards a goal that was beyond her perceptions. She was alone and determined, but of what, she was unaware. Despite her disheveled appearance, she still remained a beautiful and desirable young woman, yet there was a hardness about her. As she walked among prostitutes and winos, crack heads and huffers, she carried herself in a manner which set her apart from them. Elina was not afraid to be among them, but she had determined not to be one of them. She was not prepared to sell herself out, and she wanted to believe she would never sell out, and yet, underneath, she knew her determined independence, a characteristic once possessed by many of the people who surrounded her now, just a few disappointments ago, would carry her only so far.

Ahead of her she noticed a small line had gathered already. Since being out on the streets, after her money had run out, Elina had made a ritual of making her way toward Fannin Street and the shelter which offered daily meals. Although her pride would not allow her to stay there, she considered it wise to take advantage of the free lunch provided. She needed at least one good meal a day, and today she was glad it was a hot meal. The line would grow, and she had found through experience nothing lasted forever, so she arrived early, and waited until they were at last allowed within the shelter.

Ahead of her were two vagrants, filthily adorned in thick brown coats, their stench eking through the cold, crisp air. No doubt they were much more experienced at life on the streets than she, but she was a quick learner. This was their life, the life they had chosen, and if she didn't want to be forever a part of their world, she knew she must formulate a plan to liberate herself from its grasps.

One of the men stared at her as she approached. A growth of stubble surrounded his mouth as it opened into a broken smile; the lines in the wrinkled skin of his face were highlighted by the darkness of the dirt which had settled in them, filling in the creases, emphasizing the degradation. His voice was slurred and unsteady.

"Hey, sweetheart, want to entertain us while we wait for the place to open? You got some nice things under that sweater to show us?"

Elina returned his comments with a steely stare she had developed to offer others of his kind.

"What's wrong, you modest or something? Hey, Ben, this girl's not your average streetwalker; she thinks she's some kind of nun or something? 'Prob'ly savin' it for someone special, ain't ya honey?"

Still, Elina did not offer a reply. Her coldness left the two more frigid than the morning air and the one referred to as Ben moved to settle the mood.

"Aw, Hank, leave her alone. Can't you see she's just trying to get by like the rest of us?"

"Well, she'd get along better without that self-righteous attitude. You'd think she was one of them street missionaries, the way she keeps the goods wrapped up like she does. 'Sides I was just havin' a little fun."

They turned away from her, their attention being drawn to the bottle they shared between them. They were careful not to display it openly, if discovered they wouldn't be allowed to enter the shelter, and so they passed it secretively from one to the other. Elina kept her gaze from straying in their direction as much as was possible. Soon others began to gather, and she found herself surrounded by a shabby crowd of homeless and destitute, of which she felt no more a part than the people who operated the shelter.

As her eyes scanned the growing crowd, Elina noted that not all of those in line looked the part of homeless vagabond she'd always entertained in her mind. There was a mother with her two children standing in line. Although, she looked plain and rather ordinary, both she and her children were clean and well kept. Despite herself and her own situation, she felt compassion for this mother trying to make her way in a difficult time.

Inside, Elina stayed to herself, setting alone until the crowd forced others in her direction. She controlled the urge to devour her food, a ravenous feeling building within her. She sought to prolong her comfort from the streets as long as she could, drinking up the warmth of the room and the courteous, friendly smiles of the workers. Perhaps she might even dry before she had to leave.

She glanced around the room; there were people from all ages and ethnicities. The youngest appeared to be about eight or nine, while the oldest she could not discern. In the corner of the room there were a few families of various sizes gathered together at a large table. Some of them seemed nearly complete with both father and mother, but most of them seemed to only be mothers and their children. Elina noticed one little girl who reminded her of the child she had been only a few years ago. She caught her mind wandering back toward home and cut off the thought.

Elina turned back to the food in front of her, beef stew, mashed potatoes, and a hot roll. It smelled delicious and she began to eat, pacing herself. A few of the people who had sat down beside her were finished by then and they rose to leave. Before long she was alone again.

A young man came over to wipe down the table where they had been seated. She could tell by the way he was dressed he was one of the volunteers. He was clean-shaven and wore a white shirt that buttoned down at the collars. His dark hair was parted on the left and trimmed just above his collar line. He reminded her of the picture of her father, Dan, the one that her mother kept in the chest. She figured his age at about twenty-four.

"You're new around here, aren't you? I mean, I've only seen you here a couple of times."

She nodded and offered a weak smile. She wasn't exactly in the mood to converse, yet she didn't want to be totally rude. He had, after all, been one of the providers of her meal.

Not taking her subtle hint, he stuck out his hand.

"Hi. I'm Josh, Josh McMann."

Elina looked at his outstretched hand and hesitated slightly before raising hers to meet it. His hand was firm and warm.

"Hi, Josh," she offered simply.

"Mind if I sit down? I haven't taken a break this morning."

Elina simply shrugged her shoulders in another effort to send the message she wasn't really interested in conversation. However, this guy, Josh, didn't seem to be picking up on her hints. Still she continued to eat.

"There sure are a lot of people out there on the street. They all have different stories to tell. Some of them are just down and out because of their economic situations, others seem to be on the run from something, maybe something in their past. A lot of them work the streets, panhandling or turning tricks. Kind of sad that we can't do more for them."

He had a far off look in his eyes as if he was peering through the walls of the shelter and into their hearts. There was something warm in his voice as he spoke and she felt a sincerity which told her he meant what he said; this guy truly seemed to feel a desire to do more for the street people. Just as quickly as he had seemed to lose himself in his compassion, his thoughts seemed to return to the girl in front of him.

"I'm a part-time volunteer. I'm actually in the oil field business up in Northwest Oklahoma. I just come down here a few weeks out of the year to help out. I took a four month community service leave this year since they were shorthanded."

"Part-time, huh?" Her curiosity had gotten the best of her.

"I also work as a youth leader at a small church."

"Part-time?"

"Well, yeah. It's a small church. I volunteer."

"Is that all you do, Josh? Volunteer?"

"Uh, no. I run a business most of the time."

"What kind of business?" She couldn't help herself.

"Oilfield stuff," he responded.

"Oilfield? So are you rich, Josh?"

"I do okay."

"Just spend a little time here with the down and out for the pure fun of it?"

"Not exactly. It's just something I feel the need to do."

He paused cautiously.

"So, what's your story, if you don't mind my asking?" He ventured.

She was caught now. She'd opened the door by asking her own questions. She had to reply in some way, and if she said what she wanted to say, she wasn't sure she would be welcome here in the future.

"I'd really rather not talk about it."

He smiled.

"That's okay. I probably shouldn't have asked. How's the food?"

"Good thanks."

Her answer was short, but polite. He decided to leave her some space to continue, but she ignored it. Sensing the discomforting silence, he excused himself.

"Hey, I better get back to work, but if you want to talk sometime, just stop by. You don't have to wait until lunch."

Elina nodded and returned to her meal.

Later that evening, as she walked the lonely streets of Dallas, looking for a place to find shelter, she thought about that guy, Josh.

"What was his last name?" She asked herself. Then she muttered a reply. "Mc-something."

She was even a little upset at herself for brushing him off like she did. She knew he meant no harm, in fact he was pretty nice about it, but she couldn't open up to a complete stranger.

"McMann. Josh McMann, that was it." She remembered out loud.

Yeah, he was kind of nice, and cute, too. But he was nosey, and she shared Willie's opinion on nosey people. Besides, what business of it was his to pry into her life? She didn't need people like that around her. She didn't need anyone at all.

"...Especially, some rich corporate oil guy do-gooder." She added vocally.

Once again, Elina Pearson found herself closing the door on another person who might have otherwise added a little light into her cold, dark world, a world she felt she both wanted, and deserved.

Thirteen

The cold front had settled into the area, creating an atmosphere of aggression among the people of the streets. To those seeking shelter from the elements, even those inclined to an independent spirit, the warm confines of the shelter on Fannin Street were worth the small amount of pride they might have to swallow. However, there still remained those fiercely, self-reliant individuals (of which Elina was one) who could not accept such a blow to their pride. Among such people, territory becomes an issue of contention, even borrowed territory.

Elina was content to drift from place to place, seeking out a cozy corner or a protected doorway. She had no permanent island of refuge, no hidden box, no temporary dwelling to which she was tied, and therefore, she continued to search late into the night for a place which had not already been claimed. After a couple of run-ins with her vagrant neighbors, she finally settled down behind an office supply store. There was a concrete stairway leading into the back of the building, which made a corner against the building. Given some improvements, it would do for the night.

Elina worked quickly, breaking down several cardboard boxes to build a shelter from the frigid weather. Her bare hands were beginning to feel cold and numb. Little tasks were becoming more difficult. She flattened out the folds in the cardboard, and then she placed two of the cardboard panels above her, propping them across from the top of the steps to the dumpster nearby. Another then served as a front wall, and still two more she placed beneath her as insulation against the cold pavement below. Compared to walking the streets unprotected, Elina's little shelter seemed quite cozy.

Leaning back against the brick wall behind her, Elina began the process of settling in to her temporary home. Just as she was getting comfortable, the cardboard roof above her collapsed. She was nearly as startled as the cat that had hopped from the dumpster. As she scrambled to her feet from under the cardboard, she saw the animal scamper through what had been her front wall. Once again she setup her rickety shelter.

When at last she could settle down with her thoughts, she felt strangely drawn to thoughts of a kindly young volunteer. Elina, as much as she had tried to deny it to herself, had been touched by the actions and manners of Josh McMann. Though they had talked nearly every day since their first meeting, or at least he had talked to her, she still maintained a cool attitude in his presence. Despite that fact, he continued to carry on his conversations with a sincere and generous attitude of friendship. She had told herself it was just a ploy, a way to get into her mind and her life, but deep down she knew that wasn't true.

His gentle and enthusiastic voice had a way of melting through her hardness. Oh, she kept up the front, but he was getting in, a little at a time.

"So, where are you going to stay when the weather turns fowl?" He asked.

Elina shrugged her shoulders. "I'll find some place. There's always a place out there. I just have to look."

"Don't you get tired of moving from place to place? I mean, how long are you going to go on living like this?"

His words touched on the same questioning emotions she had been dealing with and it angered her to hear them spoken by someone else.

"Look, Josh, not that it's any of your business, but I don't have a lot of choice. I'll get along. You just worry about yourself."

He stumbled at a reply. He was trying to be cautious. He could see her anger at his questioning. It seemed each time he started to make some headway, things drifted off into turbulent waters.

"Hey, I'm not trying to make you mad. I'm gonna be leaving here in another couple of months, and I want to know you're going to be all right. That's all, okay."

She gave him a stolid look.

"Yeah, you'll be leaving our little piece of paradise shortly. You don't need to concern yourself on my account. You can go back to making money on fossil fuels and forget all about it."

The tides had turned, and it was his turn to feel the frustration rise.

"That's not fair, Elina. I do concern myself with what happens here. I pray for all of the people that pass through this place."

"Well, if you're so concerned, why do you run off to another part of the country? Why not just stay here?"

"I have another job, another responsibility, and that job allows me the funds to be able to afford taking the time to be here. I also happen to know that I can't fix all of the world's problems. I do what I can to make things better while I'm here. I accept my limitations and allow God to make up the difference."

"Well, don't worry about me, Mr. Part-Time Volunteer. I'll get along just fine."

He was struck with a moment of boldness, and in that moment, learning more about her became more important than keeping her calm.

"So, why are you here Elina? What are you running away from? Is anyone out there looking for you?"

"I told you. It isn't your concern."

"Yeah, you told me. Why won't you let me help you? You can do better than this life you're living."

Her eyes cut into him and her jaws clinched.

"I told you. It is not your concern."

With that the conversation had stalled. She tried to scare him off, and she could tell he was concerned he had pushed too far, but he was definitely getting closer, whether he knew it or not. And part of her wanted him to keep trying; she'd never admit it, but it was there.

There were times when she wished things had gone differently. Sometimes, she even imagined what it would be like if she could meet someone like him to take her away from all of this, but she knew she was past that now. She wasn't fit for someone like him. He was a gentleman, whether she admitted that to him or not. His personality proved he was meant for someone better than her. She damaged goods. She had chosen her course, and Josh McMann was just another person to meet along the streets.

Still, she allowed herself the day-dreams as she walked along and even in the night dreams, the ones that weren't nightmares; Josh McMann seemed to find a way into her thoughts. Those were the peaceful dreams; the Ozzie and Harriett, Leave it to Beaver, type dreams. She was a wife, a loving mother, her husband came home to her each day, and each night they lay awake next to one another, sharing their days and their love. In those dreams, she felt the warmth of someone beside her, but in the morning she awoke with the cold wall of her current, temporary shelter against her side.

"Why aren't you married," she'd asked him. "Is it against your religion or something?"

"No, of course not!" He replied with amusement. "I guess I never met the right person. Up until a few years ago, I was so busy with building my business I really didn't have time for a relationship. Besides, I figure that the right person will come into my life at the right time."

"You ever think about it?"

"Sometimes, I guess."

He looked somewhat uncomfortable, and Elina gained some kind of satisfaction at having put him on the spot.

"There are times when I wish I had a family, a wife, kids; you know, the whole nine yards, but I just have to be patient. Things will happen, and it will all fall into place."

He squirmed a little.

"Listen, you don't usually like to talk about this kind of stuff, what's up with that?"

She smiled slyly.

"Nothing, Oilman. Just trying to get to know you."

"Why do you do that?"

"Do what?"

"Take those digs at my profession."

"I don't."

"Yeah, you do? Is it really so hard to think that an oil guy can have compassion or want to help?"

"Well, they do have kind of a reputation for getting rich on the backs of others, not to mention what you do to the earth."

"So you're a Greenie?"

"Greenie? You mean an environmentalist? Maybe?"

"Okay. So you want to live like a cave dweller?"

"What'd you mean?"

"Those clothes you're wearing – it took energy to make them and if there is any polyester or plastic, such as buttons, they are a byproduct of oil. The food you're eating; it took diesel to plant it, harvest it, and get it to market. Look around you. There are so many parts of your life that you owe to the discovery and production of oil. People say they are environmentalist, but they travel around to their protests in vehicles which were built with energy, steel, aluminum, and plastic that depends upon oil and other fossil fuels. They run on gas and even electric cars still need fossil fuels to be produced and to be lubricated, or even charged, for gosh sakes."

"Okay, so your job is important, but it still makes you rich. That's kind of hypocritical isn't it? Being rich and making yourself feel better by being in a place like this for a few weeks a year? I mean, you can't possibly know what it's really like for someone who lives on the streets. You just come down here to sooth your conscience once a year."

"You think so, huh?"

"Yeah."

"Maybe there are some things you don't know about me. Maybe things aren't always as they seem."

"Then tell me."

"I don't come here to sooth my rich conscience, I come here to give back. I lived here as a kid."

Her face showed her confusion.

"That surprised you didn't it?"

"Yeah, I guess."

"My dad died when I was a kid. My mom tried to keep up. She worked like crazy, but we lost the house and she didn't have any family that lived near here. We ended up on the street, but Miss Annie took us in. She helped us get back on our feet and eventually my mom had enough money to get a place of our own."

"How'd you end up running your own business?"

"My mom met a guy a couple years later. He's my stepdad. He paid for my college education and helped me get an internship with Phillips Petroleum. Once I finished my degree, we went into business together doing independent contracts for the oilfield industry. He helped me fund the company. We struggled along for a while, but then when directional drilling started to take off, we found our niche. The company just took off. And now, I spend a few weeks a year helping to give back a little of the compassion that was given to me."

"Sounds like your mom must have met a great guy."

"Yeah, he is. You know, he never treated me like a stepson. He loved me like I was his flesh and blood."

"Yeah, Phillip's like that."

"Phillip?"

"My stepdad."

"It takes a special kind of guy to step into that kind of situation."

"Yeah, I guess so."

Elina became lost in thoughts, thoughts she'd rather avoid. A few minutes later their conversation ended. Lunch was finished and Elina was back out on the streets.

"Some day, maybe after I get my act together…" she'd told herself on more than one occasion. But Elina didn't really foresee someday in her future. She'd be quite surprised if she made it to her nineteenth birthday. The streets wore people down fast and unless she got out of there quickly, she'd be stuck in a place where the future simply meant finding another place to spend the night, or panhandling another meal. It wasn't the kind of life she wanted, but somehow she felt it was the kind of life she just might deserve.

She fell asleep against another stonewall. Her nightmare returned to haunt her once more. She woke with her heart racing in her chest; sweat beading up on her skin. She was at first disoriented, but soon settled down to sleep once again. This time her dreams were pleasant, even wonderfully happy; dreams of a common life.

The only streets were those quiet ones which surrounded her neighborhood, the only shadows were those cast by glorious green trees, and the only sounds were those of childish laughter. Above the skyline was broken by the lazy clouds which floated across the baby-blue sky, not the towers of glass and concrete, and below her feet, in absence of the asphalt to which she had become accustomed, lay a carpet of lush grass. The sweetness of blooming fragrances hung in the air that once held the fumes of exhaust, and Elina Pearson, alone in her dark little corner, absorbed it all, a smile forming upon her face.

Fourteen

Dawn broke through the skyline, its light bouncing off the glass panels of the high-rises, searing through the chill of the morning. Once again, Elina Pearson found herself walking the pavement, surrounded by buildings and shadows, a valley of concrete and glass, determination driving her forward. She had been on her own for nearly two months, the last eight weeks on the streets of Houston. She knew she needed to find some kind of employment if she was to continue to survive. Her shapely figure was now reduced to a thin layer of covering for her bones.

She had somehow avoided the pitfalls many young girls on the street endured, being forced into prostitution by some thug who offered to take care of her in return for her personal services. But she was growing weaker and the weariness which ensued fogged her mind; she knew it would not be long before her decision-making abilities were impaired in such a way as to make her an easy target for such scum. Yet she was determined and she was independent, in need of no one. Her survival depended solely upon her own resolve.

Elina took to the streets, but this time in a different way, she was in search of employment. She had grown tired of the nights spent between alleys, under awnings, and behind dumpsters. She felt a desperation growing, and a sense that she was nearing the end of her sanity. If she didn't improve her situation soon, she feared her resolve might begin to crumble and she would grasp at whatever options where available.

The scent of spent diesel fumes drifted upon the air at the bus terminal, as the buses awaited travelers loading and unloading, beginning trips, reaching destinations. Carts of luggage moved back and forth between the terminal and the buses, and Elina noticed that some of the people she saw at the shelter from day to day pushed those carts. They were eking out a living by tending to the travelers and garnishing tips for their services. As minimal as it might be, it was income.

Elina entered the terminal and worked her way thru the crowd towards the restrooms. There she stared into the mirror at the ghastly sight she had become. Dark circles surrounded her once radiant blue eyes; her face was drawn and sunken; her hair, which had been brushed and tended to with gentle care when she was a child, was a tangled, matted mess. In her reflection she could see a stick figure of a person, and had she known no better, she would not have recognized the person standing before her.

She turned on the sink and soaped down her face and hands. Stripping off her sweater, shirt, and bra, she soaked a wad of paper towels and scrubbed off the soil and sweat which had taken the place of perfumes and body oils. Other women entered the restroom and though a few of them seemed startled at her nakedness, most paid her no attention. There were many stranger happenings in a city like Houston, than a young vagrant woman cleaning up in a bus stop restroom. She gathered up a handful of liquid soap from the dispenser and, turning her head to the side, wet and lathered her hair. It wouldn't remove the mats or tangles, but it might bring a cleaner look to her.

She turned on the hand dryer and pointed the nozzle up into her face, trying to straighten as many tangles as she could with her bony fingers. This seemed to cause the most disruption to her companions in the restroom, as there were only two hand dryers and she kept one tied up for a long period of time, continuously hitting the switch to restart it, forcing others to use the paper towels.

When she felt she had done as much as she could with her hair, Elina put back on her bra and sweater to cover her naked top, while she rinsed out her shirt in the sink. Again she engaged the use of the hand dryer and elicited rude stares from those who felt inconvenienced by her. It took some time to dry the shirt to a point at which she could wear it once again, but it had taken on a cleaner look and Elina determined it had been worth the trouble.

Elina felt a refreshing feeling. She would rather have had a hot bath or a shower, but at least she had lost some of the stench of the streets. The view in the mirror had not changed much, skin just a little whiter, hair not quite a mess, but still she felt better. She felt she might be presentable enough to convince some coffee shop entrepreneur to give her a chance to wait tables or clean up after the customers.

But reality has a way of dampening the hopes of even the hopeless. When she went out into the real world, Elina found more than disappointment; she found rejection. There were few jobs to be had and those which were available required a permanent address or references, neither of which she could supply. When she approached a business looking for employment she was met with cold, unfeeling stares or out right disgust.

"We don't have no jobs for street walkers," one old man replied. "Now get out of here before you run off my paying customers."

When she did find some compassion in the workplace, she was faced with a wall of obstacles, business owners, having been burned by compassion and understanding in the past, were leery of hiring someone off the street.

"I understand, dear, but we've always had difficulty hiring people like you. They just stay long enough to get a few meals and then they disappear. We need people we can depend upon."

"But you can depend on me," Elina countered. "I just need to earn enough money to get on my feet and then I'll get a place of my own. How can I get a permanent address if no one will give me a chance?"

The woman shook her head. "I'm sorry, dear. I just can't take the risk. Perhaps you could check with the shelter, sometimes they place people in employment around the city."

She'd heard that all before and in the end, she found the day sending her back to where she had started, lonely, unsheltered, and cold. Elina bedded down behind an appliance store, huddled between the boxes, hidden as much as possible from the elements and from the harder elements of the street, the human elements.

In a lonely suburban home in Denton, Texas, Darcy Pearson Henning sat with her head in her hands. She'd been this way for the last two months. Though she had the companionship of her son and her husband, she longed for her daughter. Just a word, some kind of sign she was okay, would be enough to get by on, but the agony of not knowing where she was, or even if she were still alive, ate away at her, gnawing at her sanity, wearing her down bit by bit.

She feared her daughter was dead, but she held on to the slightest of hope. She questioned and reasoned to determine just what had gone wrong and why Elina had made the decision to leave. They had been relatively easy on her after the run in with the police department. Though there had been the clash at the breakfast table the morning after, it was no more violent than other mornings. They'd done nearly all they could to keep peace with her.

Phillip opened the front door. He knew in an instant that things had not changed since he left for work that morning. In a halo of light from the single lamp in the living room, he could see the bent form of his wife, he could hear her sobs and he knew Elina was still gone.

"No word, Darcy?"

She didn't reply.

"Honey, are you okay?"

Her weeping continued.

He raised his voice slightly. "Darcy, Honey, are you okay? What's wrong? Did you hear something?"

From across the darkened room, she exploded with grief.

"No! No! No! No, I haven't heard anything! No, I'm not okay! No, I'll never be okay again! Where is she?"

Phillip was stunned. He wasn't angered, he knew her expressions weren't focused at him, but they were shocking just the same. Her voice lifted into a cry of agony, and the only thing he could compare it to was the way he imagined a mother would react to learning her child had died. He reached for her, and wrapped his arms around her as she cried into his chest, her words muffled against him.

"Where...is...she? Oh, Phillip, where...is...she?

Phillip Henning stood in the middle of the darkened living room holding his wife. As her sobs lurched out in long agonizing gasps, he rubbed his hands over her back and pressed his cheek into her hair. She wasn't like this, Darcy was strong, and he had never seen her in this state before. He knew she hurt, but she couldn't go on this way. Phillip led her back over to the chair and he knelt at her side, brushing her hair with his fingers. He spoke softly, tenderly, trying to console her.

"I'm sorry, sweetheart. We'll keep looking. She's out there, Darcy. I know she's out there. We'll find her."

Darcy wiped at her eyes, her breathing was elevated, and interrupted by great, gasping shudders.

"Phillip, we don't know that. She might be dead for all we know. Why doesn't she call if she's alive? Where is she, Phillip? How could she just disappear?"

"Darcy, we can't lose hope. There are a lot of places for someone to hide out there if they don't want to be found. She could be anywhere, even across the country, by now. We just have to keep praying she's all right, Darcy. Don't give up, not yet. We can't give up yet."

A misty rain had fallen, forming a puddle on the top of the cardboard box Elina had chosen as shelter. The saturated material began to drip like a wet sponge delivering an icy trickle, which fell into Elina's hair as she slept. She tried to reposition herself to keep out of its way, but the box wasn't cooperative. Each time she moved it tried to roll, and she was afraid her movements might cause its wet and weakened structure to collapse altogether. And so, she tolerated it, and tried to force herself back to sleep.

Her thoughts were being attacked once again by the nagging feeling that she should just give up and go home. The loneliness was nearly consuming, and the fear she refused to acknowledge... well, sometimes just stifling it was enough to send her into near panic. She was a courageous girl. She always had been, even as a child. In fact, some of her child hood antics had nearly scared her mother half to death. The time when she was seven and climbed on the roof just to get a little closer to the white puffy clouds which floated by overhead was an experience her mother had found most troubling. It didn't help matters any that Darcy had always been afraid of heights herself, which made it all the more difficult to get her daughter down. Elina had been both exhilarated and fearless. However, all of her courage couldn't displace the building anxiety life on the streets created.

Suddenly her thoughts were interrupted as both she and the box lurched sideways. She felt her body roll and the wet cardboard collapsed atop of her with the jolt. She felt the rough hands reaching in for her wrists and she fought back against them. Pulling her knees up underneath her and using them as springs, she thrust upward with her shoulder meeting the soft middle of her attacker, sending him off balance and knocking him to the ground. As he struggled to his feet, she reached back into the remains of her cardboard home. Her fingers danced around quickly, until they felt the cold surface, grasping it firmly. She swung her right arm with all the power she could muster and when the steel bar met his skull, the man went down offering no indication he would rise and continue the attack.

She didn't wait to find out. As soon as she saw he was down, she ran for the only refuge of which she was aware; she ran toward Miss Anne's shelter on Fannin Street.

The Redemption of the Rose

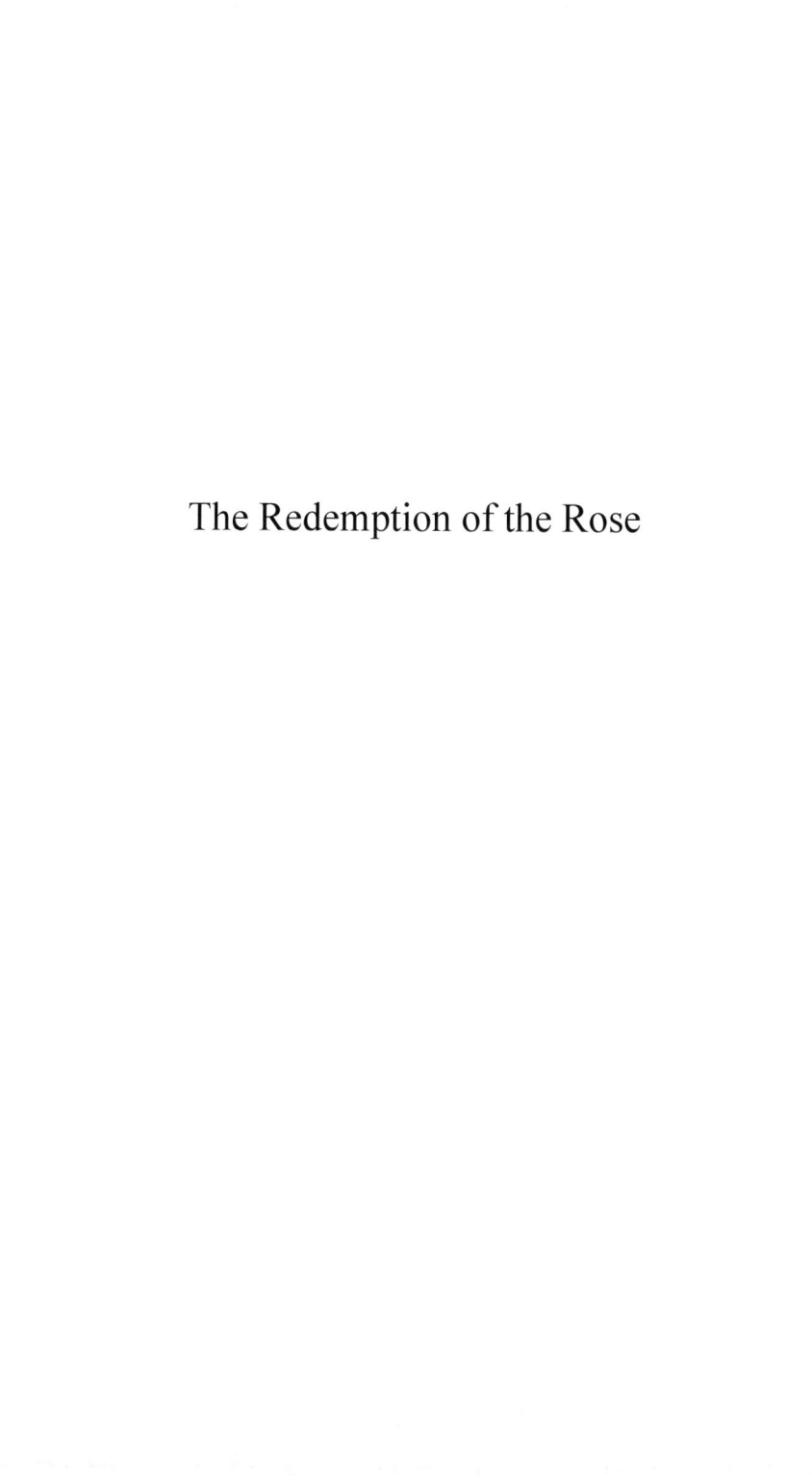

Fifteen

The smells of food, people, and city mingled just like the voices echoing in the long, open dining hall. In the shelter on Fannin Street, those who had no hope found a sliver of sunshine breaking through the day. There they received warmth and kindness, understanding and compassion. It was in that place where they sought peace from the shadows which haunted them on the streets.

Elina Pearson sat at a table in the shelter. Josh McMann was seated across from her. Although her pride told her to do otherwise, she'd come to the realization she needed some help. And after the experience in the alley, she'd felt the urgency to fix her situation. Every effort on her part to find a job had left her slipping further into despair. In her desperation, she'd turned to the only person she for whom she held any trust, Josh McMann.

"Why don't you just go home?" He asked.

"Geez, why did I come to you?" She retorted.

"I'm just saying…Look if you aren't making it on your own, why not swallow your pride and go home."

She flew to her feet.

"Because they don't want me there!" She screamed.

Nearly every head in the shelter turned her way. Miss Anne, who headed up the shelter, turned in her direction, but Josh motioned her off.

"Okay, okay. Settle down. I'm not trying to make you mad. I'm just trying to understand."

She looked around and realized she'd just created a scene. She slumped back down into the chair.

"Sorry. Look, I can't go back." She insisted.

"Why is that, Elina? Is it a bad situation? Abuse?" He quizzed.

"You wouldn't understand. I just can't."

She paused looking him square in the eyes.

"Can you help me or not?"

"I'll call a friend of mine. She will probably have something for you if I vouch for you, but you have to promise me that you'll show up for work. This isn't something I'd do for just anyone. These businesses down here have been burned too many times. They've given people a chance only to have someone who steals from them, or doesn't show up for work. Sometimes they quit as soon as they have enough money for booze or drugs. It isn't easy to get them to give someone associated with the shelter a try."

"I promise. I'll be there. I don't do drugs and I've only had one drink since I left home. It was my birthday."

"Will you stay at the shelter?"

"I can't." She said flatly.

"Why not?" He pursued.

"You wouldn't understand."

"You keep saying that, but you don't give me a chance to understand."

"It's like giving in. It's hard enough to ask you for help, but I'm smart enough to know I'm not going to get a job any other way."

"If you stayed here, you could get some rest, a shower, and clean your clothes."

"I can to that if I get enough money to get my own place."

"How long is that going to take?"

"I don't know. Maybe a month."

"A deposit, rent, utilities, food, clothes…It's going to take more than a month to get enough money for that. You're going to be able to keep a job a lot better if you are clean and well kept. This lady I'm talking about calling, she runs a restaurant. You think she wants someone who hasn't had a real bath in two months working in her kitchen?"

"No, I guess not." She admitted.

"Then stay here. I'll get you a bed. You can take a shower, wash your hair, wash your clothes…"

"What happens if I can't handle it here?"

"Then I guess you can leave."

She mulled it around. It would be nice to actually feel really clean. Her hair felt so matted she was almost sure it would have to be cut to make any order of it. Still, she felt she would be giving in; giving up her freedom.

It was as if Josh could read her mind.

"You don't have to give up your freedom to accept some help. It doesn't make you any weaker. It doesn't mean you're not strong enough."

"Okay, I guess." She said reluctantly. "As long as I can leave if I want."

"You aren't a prisoner here. You come of your own accord. You can leave at will. If you really want to get your act together Miss Anne will help you. I'll help you, but no one is going to force you to stay or to get your life together."

Josh stood.

"I'll be right back."

She watched as he walked over to Miss Anne. They spoke for a minute and then the two of them walked back to the table where she was sitting.

"Come with me Sweetheart. We'll get you set up. It ain't like you'll have your own room, but you'll have a comfortable place to sleep."

Miss Anne took Elina by the arm. Josh watched as they walked off together and he lifted up a prayer in the hopes that Elina might finally be taking a step in the right direction. She deserved a better life than this. She deserved to be with someone who loved her.

Elina gazed at the image looking back had her from the bathroom wall. The change was even more profound than the one she had experienced at the bus station. Her face was gaunt, almost like a skull with a thin film of skin over it, pale in color, nearly translucent. She'd been right about her hair. There was just no saving it. It was now cropped short, just below her ears. The long tresses she'd had since childhood were now gone and with the change in her other physical appearances, she was staring at a different person. Her mind wandered to her mother. What would she think of her right now?

That thought led to another, and soon she was scolding herself for allowing her mind to go there in the first place. She blamed the weakness on Josh and his suggestion she should stay at the shelter. Her anger seethed beneath the surface and she nearly bolted from the building. Instead, she vowed to make her stay at the shelter a short one.

In the meantime she had to go talk to a lady about a job. Josh had come through for her and if things worked out, she would soon be earning a paycheck by washing dishes in a small café downtown. In fact, if she worked out okay, the lady had offered to move her out front to wait on tables where she could make even more money.

Sixteen

Elina's work at the café seemed to be the spark she needed to get her act together. She had earned the praises of her boss for her work. With her first check, she bought some more clothes, clothes which actually fit her thin frame. She was quickly moved out to the front of the cafe and her friendly, but spunky personality had proven successful with the customers.

"Hey, Casey! Where'd you get this girl?" Tom, one of the regulars called out.

"She just wandered in one day." Casey replied with a smile. Then she winked at Elina.

"Well, you better hang on to her. She's the only reason I've been coming back.

Elina glowed in the compliments. She'd worked hard to make this opportunity for change meaningful. She still had her demons, but she had been keeping them at bay during the days. They only seemed to return during her nights. This made her relish the time she spent at work all the more.

Though she was far from where she wanted to be, self-sufficient and away from the shelter, she knew she was taking another step with each day. In a short time, she would have saved enough money to move out on her own. Her confidence was returning and her determination was rekindling.

She heard the bell on the door and turned to greet the next customer. This one got a special smile from her. Josh had been in nearly every day to see her and to be sure that things were working out. Though he still had some time left in his mission at the shelter, they seldom saw each other there. She spent most of her day at the café.

"Hey, there." He said with his trademark smile.

"Hey." She responded.

Her defenses still wouldn't allow her to admit to him that he was having influence upon her, but he was. She held on to those feelings which told her she could never be good enough for him. He deserved someone less tarnished. He had that special something about him, and would certainly be rewarded with a woman who was just as special. Someday, he would find her, that woman who could complete him, a woman who shared his compassion and understanding. Not her, not someone who carried so much baggage it would take an airline trolley to move it all.

"A Coke to get you started?" She quizzed, handing him the menu.

"Sure." He agreed.

She moved off to get his drink, while he scanned the menu.

Looking over the edge of the menu, he watched her move. He could see the young woman inside was starting to return. Confident, self-assured, the kind of girl he'd like to fall in love with some day. Though she was beautiful even at her worst, she was starting to blossom now. As her body once again started to reclaim its natural features, the elegance of the girl had begun to shine through. The luster of her blonde hair had returned and when she stepped out into the sunlight it glistened with golden highlights. Her face, once so thin that her cheekbones seemed to be nearly pushing through the surface of her skin, now accentuated her beautiful smile. Above all, her ocean blue eyes twinkled with the enthusiasm which had begun to grow inside.

He continued to admire her as she worked behind the counter, oblivious to his watchful eyes. When at last she turned to bring his drink back to the table, his eyes darted back to the menu.

She caught his glance as she turned, and it warmed her heart that he'd bothered. Though she was quick to beat back the spark it ignited, she allowed its acknowledgement for the briefest of seconds. He was just being the endearing person she had grown to know; ever watchful of her, keeping her near to his wing.

She placed the drink upon the table and he looked up at her. There was something in his eyes, something she'd never noticed before; almost as if for a moment she meant more to him than just another weary soul to which he could minister. The warmth of that thought generated through her, but again, she pushed it aside.

"What can I get you today?" She said, recovering her composure.

"I think I'll have today's special."

"Good, choice. Casey's meatloaf is to die for." She reassured him.

As she took his order to the kitchen window, he continued with his admiration. He was startled by a nudge at his shoulder. He turned to see Tom wink at him.

"Careful there Joshua, you may stumble on some less than righteous thoughts."

Josh laughed nervously at the joke offered at his expense, but Tom continued.

"It's okay. If I was your age, I'd be considering the possibilities too. That girl's a keeper."

Josh nodded.

"She certainly is." He agreed.

To occupy his time while he waited for his meal, and to distract his mind from its wandering, Josh picked up the newspaper nearby. He skimmed through the articles on the front page and found one that was of interest. Reading about the City Council's plans for dealing with the growing homeless population, he followed the article to page nine where it continued. He heard the bell at the kitchen window ring and was about to fold up the paper when something caught his eye. Taking a second glance, he suddenly recognized the face in a picture staring back at him. It was Elina.

"Denton Teenager Missing" the headline above the picture read.

He glanced back up in time to see Elina pulling his order from the window. As she turned to bring it to his table, he quickly folded the newspaper and placed it in his lap. He'd have to look at it later. With Elina at his side holding his order, he felt Tom nudge him in the shoulder once again.

"Hey, Padre, are you finished with that paper?"

"Uh, sure." He replied hesitantly, before passing it on to the old man.

"Can I get you anything else?" Elina asked after placing his meal in front of him.

"No, thank you. I'm good." He replied while trying to keep an eye on the newspaper.

She pulled the chair across from him away from the table.

"Do you mind if I sit with you while I take my break?"

"No, I don't mind at all."

Though they conversed easily and he felt warm with her attention, his mind continued to wander back to the newspaper. When he heard Tom push his chair back from the table and saw Elina rise to check him out at the register, he allowed his mind to relax for a moment. However, when he glanced up to see the man leaving with the newspaper tucked under his arm, his heart sank.

Elina returned to check on him.

"Anything else?" She asked.

He shook his head.

"Uh, no, I think I'm done."

"How was it?"

"Delicious."

She smiled.

"Told you."

She paused for a moment.

"Uh, I think I'm going to look at some apartments next week. Would you mind coming along? I'd just like to have someone else there with me. I haven't ever done anything like that and I'm not sure what I should be looking for." She explained.

"No. No, I wouldn't mind at all. Just let me know what day you want to go and I'll make sure I'm free."

"Miss Anne won't mind?"

"Are you kidding? She'll be ecstatic. She loves it when someone makes it out of the shelter."

"Great." She said, lifting with enthusiasm.

They walked together to the checkout counter.

"So, maybe I'll see you for a few minutes this evening?" Elina asked cautiously.

"I hope so." He said as he handed her the money for the meal.

"Okay, well, see you later." She offered.

He turned to leave and then paused.

"Would you like to go do something tonight?" He asked.

Stunned, Elina hesitated before answering.

"Like what?"

"Oh, I don't know. I just thought you might like to get away from the shelter for a while. Maybe we could go to a movie or something."

"Sure. Sounds like fun." She said, her smile beaming.

"Okay. We'll go after you get off work."

"What are we going to see?" She quizzed.

"Oh, I don't know. I'll take a look at the paper and see what's showing."

He paused.

"Hey, you don't have another newspaper laying around, do you? It seems Tom took off with the other one."

Elina glanced around at the tables.

"No, I think that was the last one."

He nodded.

"Okay, I'll… uh… just pick one up at the stand. I'll see you later."

"Okay." She said, trying to hide her excitement.

The remainder of the afternoon seemed to float by for Elina. She found her mind drifting toward Josh more and more often. She tried to temper her feelings, reminding herself over and over that he was just a nice guy doing his job, but the excitement persisted as much as she tried to bury it under normalcy.

When at last her shift was over, she collected her tips and rushed for the door. Though a storm had moved in, bringing with it dark and ominous clouds, it wasn't enough to dampen her spirits. Even the dreary darkness of the space between the large buildings downtown and the rain pouring down like buckets of water weren't powerful enough to wash away her enthusiasm.

Seventeen

Elina held on to her excitement as she nearly skipped through the pouring rain. She rounded the corner two blocks west of the shelter. Half way down the block, as she passed the alley, two grungy arms caught her around the waist. As she was being pulled back deep into the alley, she felt the grip of a pair of rough, dirty hands move to her wrists. The tight grasp pulled at her, dragging her body further into the darkness of the alley. Her arms stretched out behind her, pinching her shoulder blades together, a pain shot through her neck as she was jerked from behind. As much as she struggled, she couldn't make out the image of her captor.

She screamed at the top of her lungs.

"Let me go! Let me go! Help me! Somebody, help me!"

Her shouts had no effect upon her assailant.

On down the alley they went, Elina screaming and kicking, her abductor silent and determined. One hand broke free and with it she clutched for anything she could hang onto, for anything she could throw or use as a weapon. She felt the seat of her pants tear upon the pavement, and then it was bare skin burning as the concrete tore it away. Her head banged into the side of a dumpster, and it began to throb with the pace of her pulse. And then, everything went dark.

When she aroused she could feel his presence over her, she could smell that familiar stench, and she recognized the voice immediately.

"You think you're pretty uppity, don't you girl? Wouldn't even give me the time of day when I spoke to you! Then that night I come to visit you, you darn near whacked my head off with that bar. I had a goose-egg the size of Texas for three days. Well, we'll just see how much time you give me now."

She struggled to swing at him, but her wrists wouldn't cooperate. As she strained to move, she felt the cloth he had restrained her with, pull against her wrists. They were tied to something, something cold and metal, a rail or a fence of some kind. She tried to kick at him instead, but her legs didn't move either. It took her a moment to realize, through the fog in her head, that he was sitting on her legs.

"Don't touch me!" She screamed.

He seemed amused.

"Don't touch me!" He mocked. "Girl, when I get through with you, you're gonna be touched all over. Now, let's see what you were hidin' under that sweater."

"No, please!" She pleaded, but he stuck his wretched mouth against hers to silence her words. His stubble scratched at her face, his smell was sickening. To fight back, she bit at his lip.

He swung his hand fiercely into her cheek.

"You're gonna pay extra for that. Ol' Ben thought you was some kind of innocent. He said we shouldn't ought to bother you, because the streets was gonna git you first. Well, wait 'til I tell ol' Ben that I got a little piece of you before the streets got it all."

"Please don't hurt me."

"Oh, I don't guess it's gonna hurt much, or at least not for long. 'Sides you might even like what ol' Hank has to offer. You be good now. No more of that bitin' and kickin' and I might just let you go when I'm done with you. Ain't nobody gonna help you out here in this rain anyway. Ain't nobody around, and if there was they'd just figure you got what you deserved. You're just street trash. There ain't no one gonna bother helping street trash."

Elina was quiet, still stunned by the blow to her face. Her left eye was swelling quickly; she could tell by the way it was affecting her vision. She was scared, more scared than she had ever been. That small quiet voice she had so long tried to squelch, the one that tried to tempt her to give up her freedom and return home, was now screaming at her, reminding her that she should have listened.

Hank spoke again, a little softer, as if he was trying to win her favor. The smell of liquor and cigarettes on his breath was fowl, and it disgusted her to think of what he was about to do to her, but she kept silent and still, hopeful she might live through the ordeal she was facing.

"You sure are a pretty thing. Even nicer now that you're all cleaned up. It wouldn't bother me none if you weren't though. Hell, look at me. I been out here so long, I can't remember the last time I slept with a whole roof over my head."

His rough hand was caressing her arms, and he had a far away look in his eyes, as he looked back through his past. Suddenly he snapped back.

"Well, now, let's just have a look under that blouse there…"

As he started unbuttoning her top, she began pleading with him once again, squirming to evade his plans.

"No, please." She whispered. "Please don't."

A thought came into her mind.

"I've got some money. I'll let you have it if you let me go."

"I already found that while you was out cold."

As hard as she tried to fight them back, she felt the tears filling her eyes. She stared at him, her vision blurring. Her voice rose in pitch, but it was still just a whisper.

"Don't do this. Please, leave me alone."

This only seemed to anger him. He hit her again and again with his closed fist. She felt the pain in her jaw.

"I told you to keep quiet! I tried to go easy on you, but you wouldn't let me! Now, we'll do it my way!"

With that, he yanked down at her collar, ripping her top open, sending the buttons flying into the darkness of the alley. She felt the large cold drops of rain against her exposed skin; the frigidness of the air which blew over her dampened flesh chilled her to the bone and her smooth, youthful skin turned to a pathway of goose bumps.

"Aw, that was something special you was hiding under there." Hank said, his eyes showing the lust and admiration growing inside of him.

His dirty, grungy hands moved over the white lace cups of her bra. Then he grabbed it at both sides and ripped it away as well, exposing her to his lust filled eyes.

She was trembling from both the cold and the fear growing within her. A shudder went through her body, shaking her violently when she felt his rough hands against her. Her trepidation rose as she felt the grubby fingers trail down her torso, pausing just a moment at the top of her jeans.

The thought of his dirty hands, the nasty thoughts in his mind, and the images of what he was about to do to her caused her stomach to churn and she felt the bile rising in her throat. She smelt his stench as he moved closer to her and her nausea grew. When she felt the top button of her jeans pop open, her body froze and her mind drifted away.

She was back in her dream, the dream she so often had as a child. She was wearing that little pink dress, the one which had been her favorite. They were in the park, she and her mother. From behind her she heard a voice call her name. Turning to face it, she saw Daddy Dan standing beneath an oak tree. His face was just as kind and gentle as he had always seemed in his pictures. He was smiling at her and holding out his arms.

"Elina. Come to Daddy, Elina. Come here sweetheart."

She turned to look at her mother. Her mother smiled and nodded her approval.

Elina began to walk towards him cautiously, and then, feeling the growing excitement at the possibility of being held in her daddy's arms, she began to run. On and on she ran, faster and faster, harder and harder, but the more she ran the farther away her father seemed to be. She ran until she was out of breath, and her side began to ache. Still, she could not get to Daddy Dan.

She heard her own voice pleading.

"Please..Please..."

She continued on, though exhausted, barely able to take each step. And just when she thought she might reach him, he lifted his hand in a wave, and then disappeared.

The little girl in her apparition fell to her knees; lifting her white-gloved hands to her face, she cried. It was always the same, always so close, but never enough. Just when she thought she might reach him, just when she thought she might feel the love which had been missing in her life, he simply went away. Her weeping grew louder and louder until she cried out all that was within her, until her painful cries eroded into a quiet whimper.

Josh rushed franticly down the sidewalk. He'd made the trek once already. She'd left the café right after her shift. This time he was searching the hidden corners of his path. A quiet echo slid up the alley nearby. He paused. Once again, the quiet whimper echoed against the brick walls. He turned around and stepped closer, to listen once again. He headed down the darkened alley toward the sound. He was almost tossed off his feet by the rough looking character who ran past him as he entered the alley.

Peering closer, he saw her, naked against the cold wet pavement, her hands still bound, only the quiet whimper giving any indication of life. Her skin was cold to the touch, but at least she was alive. He unbound her wrists. The cloth had worn deeply into her skin, and her hands had a purple tint to them. Her face was bruised and swollen, her left eye nearly shut. Removing his jacket, and placing it over her, he slipped the cell phone from the inner pocket.

When the ambulance arrived, followed closely by the police, he remained to watch as they worked to save her. While the detectives questioned him, he gazed after the flashing lights transporting her. And when at last they were finished with him, he followed her.

Eighteen

Time passed slowly. With each passing hour he wondered when she would wake. It had been nearly forty-eight hours since she had come in suffering from both hypothermia and the abuse she had taken. Her face was bruised and swollen, her body scratched and violated. He felt an enormous sorrow for what she had been through, and yet a deeper sorrow for the fact that she was there without her family beside her.

How could such a beautiful girl end up like this? What had happened in her young life to leave her out on the streets alone? They were, for now, the unanswerable questions. All he could do was wait and hope that somehow he could help her to find her way.

When Elina opened her eyes, the first face she saw was that of Josh McMann. He had stayed by her side from the moment she was wheeled into the room. He felt connected to her in someway, and he wanted her to know someone cared.

"Where am I?" Her raspy voice roused him from his sleepy state.

He leaned forward and took her hand.

"You're in the hospital. You've been here a couple of days. Do you remember what happened, Elina?"

She looked away.

"I think so."

The room was quiet except for the sounds of the monitors. He could feel the shame in her voice, and he knew he had to find a way to reassure her that she didn't deserve what had happened to her.

"How did I get here?" She was still unable to look into his eyes.

"I found you in an alley. You were in pretty bad shape."

"You found me?"

"Yes."

"So you saw me like that?"

"Yes."

She turned her head once again, in anguished embarrassment. She was ashamed of the thought that her nakedness had been exposed to him, to the world for that matter, but especially to him in such a way. She didn't know how many people had seen her like that, the others didn't really matter. She didn't know them, but he knew what had been done to her. It made her feel dirty.

Of course, he had seen her unclean and unkempt, yet that had little effect upon her. He knew she'd lived on the streets; it made her feel tough. But somehow the thought that he knew what that man had done to her, that he had seen her naked, ravaged body, that he had images in his mind of the act which had been forced on her, made her feel like vomiting. She couldn't control her stomach, or push back the lump in her throat.

He handed her the tray next to her bed. He didn't turn away from her as the bile forced its way up. He put his head on her forehead, and wiped the sweat from her brow with a wet cloth. He pulled her hair back away from her face, and he helped her when she tried to lie back down. He showed no fear, no anxiety, and no repulsion. He was definitely different from any guy she had met before.

"Elina, do you know who did this to you?"

"Yes. But it doesn't really matter."

"Of course it matters, Elina. He hurt you. You didn't deserve that."

"Hurt? You mean raped? You can say it."

His face showed his compassion.

"I'm sorry. He raped you. But if you know who it was, then they can catch him. He ran away as I got to the alley. I didn't get a good look at him; otherwise they would already be looking for him."

Her eyes strayed away.

"I told you, it doesn't matter."

"Why? Why doesn't it matter? You didn't deserve that."

She snapped back, a fury grew in her eyes.

"You don't know me! You don't know who I am or what I've done! You don't have any business telling me what I deserve!"

He was undaunted. He had seen this before. He'd experienced people like Elina; people who thought they were so worthless, so lost, that nothing could save them, and even if they could be saved, they felt they didn't deserve it. They were his reason for being there. They were part of his job. This was his ministry, his way of giving back. But there was more. This girl, this young woman, was deeply disturbed. She held on to something, she allowed it to punish her, and she didn't want to let go.

"Elina, you're right, I don't know you as well as I would like to, and I don't know what you have done that would allow you to feel you deserve what has happened to you. But I do know nothing, nothing in the world, gives someone else the right to take away your dignity, your self-esteem, and your soul without your consent. I know that no one has the right to violate you and your body the way he did. I know whatever you feel you have done, whatever you feel is so terrible about you it would make you consider yourself deserving of this treatment, can't possibly be as bad as you imagine it to be. And I know I would really like to get to know you, if you would allow me the opportunity."

She turned away from him once again.

"It doesn't matter."

Elina stared off into the distance, Josh McMann waiting patiently at her side. He wouldn't push her. He would wait as long as it took for her to soften, giving her the opportunity to share the hurt she carried. The room remained silent, and her gaze remained far off and distant, until her eyes grew heavy, and she drifted off into sleep once again.

The clock on the wall ticked quietly away at the minutes and hours which passed. Still, he waited and wondered about this beautiful young girl, and the demons which tormented her in her dreams. How could something so lovely be so dark and alone? It was obvious she was a runaway, but what had she ran from? What could have happened in her life that would steal her desire for a better life?

The nurse entered the room to check her vitals.

"Has she stirred?"

"Just for a few minutes. She didn't have much to say."

She nodded

"If she wakes up, there is an officer who would like to talk to her."

"I'll tell her, but I don't think she'll talk."

"Are you a friend?"

"I'm trying. I work at the shelter where she is staying."

"Oh, I see. Well, let us know if she stirs."

The nurse closed the door behind her.

Outside the drizzle which had fallen for the past few days continued. The sky was dark and overcast. In the hospital room, the gloom seemed to cross through the windowpane and into the room.

He watched the second hand move upon the clock. He stared out the window as the dreary light of the day began to slip away, giving in to the coming evening. He paced the floor as the minutes and hours slowly passed. When the officer checked back in, he just shook his head. She didn't stir when the nurse came in to change the bag hanging above her bed or when she checked her vitals.

He had no idea what kind of thoughts were passing inside her head. He didn't know how many times the scene replayed itself. When she once again dreamed the dream which had become etched into her mind, he sat silently by her side. As the thoughts of moments and years which had passed between her and her mother resurfaced, as the screaming and yelling at Phillip echoed in her ears, he read from the bible at her side.

As he grew tired of reading, he began dozing, twisting restlessly in the chair near her bed. There was something about this girl. An attachment had been formed on his part, and he felt it necessary to stay with her. He knew only her first name, and very little more. He thought he'd had a lead, but the newspaper he'd seen had been an old one. When he went to the newsstand, he'd been unable to find what he was looking for. All he really knew was that she was here and she was alone.

He was unaware that in a suburb just a short drive away from Dallas, a mother ached for the loss of her daughter. He had no idea what the pain of the past few months had done to her, but if he could see her at that moment, there would be no doubt. For at that moment, Darcy Henning was nearing her end.

Nineteen

It had been nearly four months since she had left. She just seemed to disappear. Not a sign, not a call, and not a trace of Elina had surfaced. Darcy's life had seemed to freeze. Nothing changed around her.

Darcy picked up the empty cup and carried it to the kitchen. Phillip had left for work after gulping down his coffee. He hurried Danny along so he could drop him off at school on his way to work. A quick kiss on the cheek and she was alone, once again.

Darcy hadn't worked a day since Elina's disappearance. Everyone around her had encouraged her to go back to work to take her mind off of things, and Darcy had even considered it, but she just had not been able to do that. It would be like admitting Elina was never going to return, and life would go on as usual. She had forced herself to behave that way when Dan died, but that was different. Dan was dead, not missing, and she had been forced to get her act together, in order to care for her daughter.

The lonely ache for her daughter had eaten any sense of purpose from her heart, and the only purpose she found these days was in her search for Elina. Now her days were spent down at the police station, posting signs, and looking for clues as to her daughter's whereabouts. She drove around the area, looking into the faces of the homeless and destitute, hoping she might find that one familiar face returning her gaze. She had driven back and forth between Denton and Dallas covering as many places as possible, but nothing had surfaced.

She had contacted missing children's organizations. She had put up posters in every place she could imagine—hospitals, churches, police stations, on telephone poles, even at Wal-Mart. They had taken out ads in newspapers. She'd searched the internet. Other than a couple of calls which turned out to be pranks, there was nothing. She had called Elina's friends, classmates, and teachers so many times she could feel their annoyance with her. Her hope seemed to be running out.

And now, fearing the worst was all she could expect, she was allowing the depression she had kept at bay to crowd in upon her. She knew the effects of depression. She knew the deep, dark crevasses of her mind, and just how far away from the living it could take her, but she was tired of fighting back against it. She had never been this far before, not even when Dan died. There was always something which pulled her back away from the edge. Often that something was Elina, but now Elina was gone. It was time to make a decision.

It wouldn't be easy, but she couldn't go on this way. She was no good to Phillip or Danny. She was no good to herself. There just simply wasn't any reason to keep living in this isolated world anymore. It had to end one way or another.

She went into the bathroom and started the tub. With the sound of the water splattering against the surface of the tub in the background, she moved over to the sink. The steam from the hot water rose into the air, creating a fog which began to fill the room. Darcy stood in front of the mirror, and stared at her image as the condensation slowly wiped it out from her view. Her robe fell from her bare shoulders and floated to the floor, leaving her body naked. It was easier than exposing the feelings which consumed her.

She moved as if in a trance, slowly, methodically. She raised the scissors to her neckline. She felt the cold metal against her skin. The sound of their snip echoed in her mind as the blades sliced thru their target. Darcy watched as her hair fell to the floor. She felt the locks as they brushed against her bare skin dropping at her feet. She felt the warmth of the pile of hair on her toes. Gathering her courage, she lifted the scissors and snipped at a spot near her neck. She looked in the mirror at her fading image. It was done.

She reached out to the clouded mirror and drew her index finger over its surface; writing out the words which must be said. Then she opened the bottle and poured its contents into her hand.

"That should be enough," she thought.

She stepped into the tub, easing down into the water. Darcy felt the relaxing warmth of the water against her skin. She plugged the overflow drain with a washcloth. With the water still running, she emptied her hand and reached for the glass of wine she had set on the stool near the tub, gulping nearly half of it. Then Darcy Pearson

Henning leaned back against the tub, allowing the water to climb over her body, and closed her eyes to shut out the world. As the steam filled the room, and the tears rolled down her check, she whispered.

"I'm ready."

Twenty

Josh McMann had slipped quietly out of the room. His eyes were heavy and his neck was stiff. He was in dire need of a cup of coffee. It had been nearly sixty hours since they had brought Elina in, and, other than their short conversation, she had stirred very little. A few times he thought he had heard her speak in her sleep, but he was unable to understand her words. It sounded like a name, but he wasn't sure.

In the waiting room he poured himself a cup of dark, black coffee.

"Looks like this has been here a while." He mumbled to himself. Taking a sip he verified his conclusion. He shrugged his shoulders at the understanding smile of a lady knitting in the corner.

"At least it's caffeine." He spoke that out loud, and she nodded.

Josh paced the room, trying to loosen his stiff body. He rolled his head from side to side and stretched his neck muscles. He wasn't in the mood to sit any longer, so he stepped out in the hallway where he could wander around a bit. Around him he could hear the beeps of monitors in various rooms, and he felt a strong urge to share with others who needed him. Perhaps when Elina was doing better, he could make his rounds about the floor.

At the end of the hall he found a prayer room. He glanced inside. It was small, but cozy. Not as stiff as some he had seen. He never really understood why those rooms were often decorated and furnished in ways which seemed to make it more uncomfortable for people to lift up their cares. He supposed it had something to do with the reverence that was expected there, but he had always felt God wanted people to be comfortable with coming to him.

Across the hall there was a bulletin board which held various announcements, and at one end was a place for the public to post their own notices. He glanced over them. Thank you notes seemed to be the most dominant form of communication. As he stared at the board a thought struck him. In the lobby there was another bulletin board, he remembered seeing it as he entered the hospital. If his recollection was correct, there might have been some missing persons posted there. Perhaps, just perhaps, this girl's family had posted some kind of missing poster in area hospitals.

Josh gulped down his coffee, making a bitter face, and headed for the elevator.

She opened her eyes and looked around the room. She was alone. He was gone. Once again she had driven someone who cared away from her. Her disappointment at his absence hit her hard. She had hoped he would still be nearby. She didn't know why she should have expected him to be there. She hadn't been all that receptive to him during their last conversation. In fact, she hadn't been receptive to him since she first met him, and that was one reason why she didn't understand his continued attempts at friendship.

Still, she had hoped he would remain by her side, even though she felt she didn't deserve it. The hardness in her tried to take over again, that part of her which wanted to believe she needed no one, but she was tired of listening to that part of her mind. It constantly told her she didn't deserve happiness. She heard the whispers which had always haunted her. They told her she was dirty. They accused her of being selfish and hateful. They made her painfully aware of the fact that she had been responsible for the death of the one person who could have pushed all this hatefulness away. If her daddy had lived, she would have been a different person. But he hadn't lived. He had died because she had chosen to enter this world at the wrong time.

The bitterness tried to rear its ugly head, but Elina was tired of listening. She had listened to those voices all of her life. They had chastised her and condemned her for as long as she could remember. She wanted them to go away. She wanted them to leave her alone, alone with those who loved her.

It was time for all of that to end. It was time to let go. It was time to let someone in. She was tired of the struggle, tired of the loneliness, and tired of the anger which had become her life. She was afraid, and finally able to admit it.

She was afraid of being alone, and yet she had only been as alone as she had made herself feel. Though she had been surrounded by love all of her life, she had kept it out. She had kept them out.

She thought of all the times her mother had attempted to break through the stone wall she had built between them. She thought of Phillip and of all of the hurtful things she'd said to him through the years. Still, he tried to love her. She thought of her brother and of the love she secretly held for him. It was a love she could not show, because it would weaken the wall. How could she have been so hateful?

She began to realize the basis of her real fear. She feared taking the chance on love only to have it taken way. She'd lost her father before she ever got a chance to know him. She was afraid of losing another person in her life, and that fear had kept her from taking the chance. If she didn't love them, then it wouldn't matter if they went away. She had tried to shut out the world. She had tried to pretend she had no fear, and look what it had gotten her. Her spirit was broken, her life was a shambles, and her body was used.

Those thoughts and so much more raced through her mind. They welled up within her, and overpowered her until she could no longer fight them back. For the first time in such a long time, she could feel the emotions building within her. They rushed forward in the form of tears, sorrows, and prayers.

Between her sobs, she cried out in quiet whispers. "Please, God. Please, let him come back. I'm tired of running away. I'm tired of being strong. I just want someone to love me and take care of me."

Moments later, Josh McMann rushed into her room with a piece of paper, a piece of paper with her picture printed upon it.

She sat up and reached out to him. And he went to her; placing his arms around her, he allowed her to cry out into his chest. He held her as her body cast off the fear and anger in violent sobs. He prayed for her with words lifted silently in his mind. She was close, so close, and he wanted her to be able to complete her journey from the dark world in which she had been hiding. He heard her whisper through her tears.

"Josh, I want to go home. I just want to go home."

He kissed her head and held her tight. He heard his voice as he spoke to her.

"Elina, they want you to come home. They want you back. They've been looking for you all along. It'll be okay, but you don't have to go it alone. There are others who will help you, if you'll let them."

She pressed her face into his shoulder.

"I'm a bad person, Josh. There are things you don't know about me, things that no one knows. How can anyone love me?"

"What have you done that keeps you from letting people love you?

"I've been hateful, and hurtful. I've said things. I've rebelled against them. My mother, my stepfather, and my brother—I've been mean to them all. And whether they admit it or not, I know they think I killed my father, and they're right. It was my fault he died. If it weren't for me he would still be alive."

He stared at her in disbelief.

"How did you kill your father Elina?"

She was crying and it made it difficult for her to speak.

"I killed him, Josh; he was coming to see me, and he died. He was trying to get to the hospital when he crashed. If it hadn't been for me, if I hadn't been born he wouldn't have been in the accident, and he wouldn't have died."

Beginning to understand the guilt she had tormented herself with, Josh took her hand.

"Elina, I'm sure it was an awful burden to grow up knowing your father was killed at the time of your birth, but that doesn't make it your fault. You weren't driving the car when your father died, he was. And you didn't choose when you would be born, God did. The timing of the two, however tragic it might have been, was not related. It was simply an accident, and you can't go through life blaming yourself for something that was not in your control. God loves you Elina, and your family loves you. See this paper? They've been looking for you. They want you to come home."

She looked at the paper in his hand. There was her picture and her stepfather's cell phone number. And at the bottom: "Elina we love you."

"I want to go home, Josh. But I've pushed them away. You don't know how I've treated my mother and my stepfather. I've been so hateful to them. How could they ever forgive me?"

Josh held her hands in his.

"Because, Elina, when you love someone, that's what you do. You forgive them, and they forgive you. That's what love is all about. It means that no matter what you do, no matter what you say, those people closest to you will always love you. Elina, I'll call your parents and tell them where you are, if you'll let me."

She nodded, and he rose to go out to the nurses' station.

Twenty-One

His wife had seemed especially quiet that morning. It seemed as time passed the relationship between them grew more strained. He loved his wife dearly, and he knew Elina's absence was wearing on her, but they still had each other, and they still had Danny to think about.

He would never give up looking for her. As long as Darcy held on to any hope, he would be right by her side, but they had to go on. He knew she didn't see it the same way; she felt she had to put every ounce of her energy into finding Elina, but he knew they had to find a way to hold on to what they had at the same time. They weren't being fair to Danny, and they weren't being fair to each other if they continued to put their lives on hold.

The traffic was light that morning. He had gotten an early start, although dropping Danny off had slowed him down a little.

He smiled as he thought of his son. He was such a chatterbox, especially that morning.

"I can't wait for recess." He confided.

"Why's that?"

"We're gonna play dodge ball."

"You like that game huh?"

"Yeah, you get to hit people with the ball."

"Sounds a little violent."

"It's just a game."

"A game where you get to hit people?"

"Yeah, cool huh?"

He shook his head. The kid deserved to have a family that wasn't nuts.

The sound of the phone startled him, but he still managed to grab it on the first ring.

"Hello."

"Hello, Mr. Henning?"

"Yes, this is Phillip Henning."

"Mr. Henning, My name is Josh McMann. I am a volunteer at the shelter on Fannin Street in Houston. I was calling you to talk to you about your stepdaughter."

He checked the rearview mirror then quickly pulled his car to the side of the road. His hands shaking as he placed it in park and turned on his hazards.

"You have some information about Elina? Is she…is she alright?"

"Well, sir, Elina is going to be okay, but she is in a hospital in Houston right now. She asked me to call you."

"What happened?"

"Sir, I'd really rather she tell you about that. She has been through quite an ordeal. I'm sure she will need some counseling, but she will be okay. Can I tell her that you are coming to see her?"

"Yes. Yes, you can. I'll stop by and pick up my wife. We'll be there as quick as we can."

"Okay, sir. I'll tell her."

"And Mr. McMann?"

"Uh, that's Josh. Yes sir?"

"Josh, thank you for calling. We've been worried sick about her."

"I'm sure you have sir. You're welcome."

As he hung up the phone, Phillip was still shaking. He took a couple of deep breaths and dialed the house. Four rings. Five rings. No answer. Strange, Darcy didn't say anything about going out this morning. Phillip pulled the car into a parking lot to turn around. She had been awful tired lately; perhaps she was taking a nap.

Elated that this long ordeal would soon be over, Phillip Henning headed for home.

He dialed the office to let them know he wouldn't be in.

"Stacy, this is Phillip. Hey, something came up and I won't be in this morning…. No, you better cancel my appointments for this afternoon as well…. Someone found Elina…. Yeah, I can't wait to tell Darcy."

Twenty-Two

Josh McMann pushed "end" on his phone after speaking with Phillip Henning. The voice on the other end had sounded concerned and relieved. He seemed nice enough, and certainly gave no hint he would be anything but happy to have his stepdaughter back safe and sound. It was nearly ten o'clock in the morning, and if all went well, Elina would be reunited with her family in a few hours. He felt good about that, and he eagerly relayed the conversation with her stepfather to Elina.

"Elina, he sounded so relieved to hear you were okay. 'Sounds like a really nice man."

She nodded.

"He is, and I've been perfectly awful to him most of my life. I remember one time when we spent the weekend in Kemah, he took us out sailing. It was one of the most wonderful weekends I've ever experienced. I love the beach; listening to the waves, feeling the warm sand between my toes."

Josh smiled at her recollections.

"He told me he'd stop by to pick up your mother, and they would both be here as soon as they could."

"My poor mother; she must have been worried sick the last few months. I can't believe they could ever forgive me for what I've put them through."

Josh shook his head.

"They'll forgive you. They'll be so happy to see you; all of the experiences of the past will disappear from their thoughts."

"Did you tell them what happened?"

"No. No, I didn't. I didn't feel it was my place. I simply told him you had been through quite an ordeal and would probably need some counseling. There are some people I can recommend, but you have a lot you need to work out, Elina."

She was quiet, and reflective.

"Josh, I never thanked you for finding me, and for being my friend, even when I wasn't so friendly to you."

She touched his hand.

"You're welcome."

"Why were you so persistent? I mean most people would have just written me off."

"Well, first of all, that's my job. It's my ministry."

"Part-time." She interjected.

He laughed.

"Yeah, part-time. Anyway, I'm supposed to look after people."

Elina waited for him to continue.

"And, well, I guess I just wanted to get to know you."

She rubbed her fingers along his.

"So, do you think we can keep in contact? I mean would you mind?"

"Would I mind? Of course not. I'll only be here for a couple more weeks and then I'm headed back home, but I'm sure we can work something out."

"Josh, do you think I could help down at the shelter when you come back next year?"

He looked stunned.

"You sure you want to do that?"

"Josh, there are a lot of people out there like me. If I can help them, maybe it will help me."

"Sure. I can arrange it. But I think you should work through some of this first. Don't take on too much too quickly."

He rubbed his hand through his disheveled hair.

"How long have you been here? You look tired." She quizzed.

"I've been here since you came in, but I'm okay. I am kind of hungry."

She smiled. It was the first time in quite a while.

"Go get something to eat. I'll be alright."

He stood up.

"Would you like something?"

"No, they'll probably bring me something in a little while. Besides, I think there is a police officer I need to speak with. Could you call him for me?"

"Sure." He patted her shoulder. "Are you up for it?"

"It has to happen sooner or later. If I talk to him now, maybe they can get him off the street before he does this to someone else."

"Okay. Your parents should be on their way."

"Josh? You will come back wont you? I would like you to meet my parents."

"Wild horses couldn't drag me away."

Phillip Henning pulled into his driveway. Darcy's car was still parked where it had been when he left. He hurried to the door. He searched the kitchen and the den. She wasn't there. He headed for the bedroom. He heard the water running in the bathroom.

As he opened the door, a misty fog flooded out into the bedroom. In the mirror in front of him he saw the message she had written with her fingertip. He saw the bottle on the counter, and the hair in the floor. Through the shower curtain, he could see the dark figure of his wife lying still in the tub. He moved cautiously toward the tub and drew the curtain back.

He looked down at his lovely wife, her naked body just beneath the pale pink colored bathwater. Her face was calm and serene, the image of a person who was finally at peace. He felt his eyes begin to fill with the tears he'd held back since the moment he received the call from Josh McMann. She was as beautiful as the first day he'd met her; the true love of his life. His eyes traced the outline of her shape. He took in the lovely dark lashes of her closed eyes.

As he stared down at her still image, he thought about the pain she'd carried with her over the past few months. He considered the strength it must have taken to make it this far and the thoughts behind the conclusion she had come to in the words she'd written on the mirror. Of course, he'd been there for her. He had shared the pain, but as much as he had tried to claim Elena as his own, she'd come from within her mother and only Darcy could feel that ache of the broken bond between mother and child.

They'd endured such a long journey together to find themselves in this place and in this moment. Now it had all come to an end, an end which was almost unimaginable just a few hours earlier. He felt as if suspended in time, split between the need to remember this moment and a desire to erase it from his memory. He knew the stinging pain of hurt and loss would one day wash away, to be replaced with memories of happier times, but in the here and now they were undeniably present.

He shook off the melancholy and knelt beside the tub. His hand stretched out and stroked the silky stray strands of hair away from her face, feeling the cool soft texture of her cheek beneath his fingertips.

She stirred, a slight smile forming on her face.

"Did you use enough of that bath salt?"

She opened her eyes and looked up at his foggy figure..

"It's rose. 'Kind of strong isn't it?"

"Yeah, just a little. Are you almost done? We really must be going."

"Going where? What are you doing home anyway?"

Handing her a towel to rush her along, he continued.

"I got a call from a shelter in Houston. Are you ready for this?" He paused to watch her eyes. "They found Elina."

"Where is she?" She asked, her eyes wide with hope.

"She is at the hospital."

Panic displayed on her face.

"Don't worry. He assured me she was going to be okay."

She rose to her feet, water flowing off her skin and beading up to form droplets on her surface. He couldn't help but notice the goose bumps which had risen over her body, her arms, legs, and breasts, turning the smooth tissue into a pebbly texture. Under other circumstances he might have taken the time to explore those little bumps with his lips, but with the excitement of his news, he allowed the moment to pass with little more than a passing thought.

"She wants to come home. Darcy, she *wants* to come home!"

He watched for a moment as her mind processed the information. Then he drew her up into his arms, pulling her close in one of his big bearlike hugs. After a moment, he stepped back, his arms extending and his hands upon her bare shoulders.

"Wow, you finally got the nerve to cut your hair, Elina will love it."

Darcy Pearson Henning stood motionless, wrapped in the towel Phillip had handed her. She had, at last, received the answer to her prayers. Her daughter was coming home. She glanced up at the mirror. Though the letters were fading as the moisture dissipated, she could still see the words she had written with her fingertip.

"I must have faith, and I must go on."

Twenty-Three

It was a reunion to rival any before it. Mother, daughter, step-father huddled together; all thoughts of the past removed from their minds. Love has a way of covering the sins and hurts; leaving only the deep, meaningful bond which unites family as one. Elina had changed over the months she'd been out on her own, but the change which mattered most took place inside of her.

A passion had been ignited within her. Having lived on the streets she'd found a purpose for being which had eluded her. The little girl who had felt she was the catalyst for her father's death, learned to look past the pain and focus on hope. It began with forgiving herself. The guilt she'd carried so long gave way to her understanding of the love which had always been there for her.

"So, you'll call later?" She quizzed.

"Of course."

"So, were you going to ask for my number?" She asked with a hint of apprehension in her voice.

He shook his head smugly.

She looked disappointed.

"You weren't?"

"Don't have to; I already have it. I called your folks, remember?" He said with satisfaction.

"Oh, geez, I forgot."

He chuckled, but the amusement was short lived when they found it was time for her to leave. After she was gone, he felt the emptiness of her leaving upon his heart. There was a sudden, almost tragic, void; it was something he didn't expect to feel so profoundly. He gazed after the car as it moved away from him, wondering just how he'd get past those feelings until he had the chance to see her again.

Their first date had been callously interrupted. They could have allowed the despicable events of that night to keep them apart. No one would have blamed them; it was understandable. Fortunately for both of them, they didn't. It wasn't easy. She still felt unworthy of others. She was stained, impure; those feelings weren't easy to overcome, but Elina was determined to recover her life.

"Hey." She answered when she saw his name on the caller id.

"Hey." He replied.

"How are you doing?" She asked trying to keep from blurting out what she really wanted to say.

"I'm okay, I guess. It's been kind of lonely here without you."

"Lonely? You have hundreds of people around you every day."

"None of them are you." He admitted.

"Aw, that's so sweet. How could you have guessed that's exactly what I wanted to hear?"

They made up for that first date a few months later. They met in Houston near the shelter one summer weekend. The weather was beautiful and when she pulled up in that dark blue convertible, the light shimmering off both its polished surface and the lenses of her sunglasses, she reminded him of one of those California girls. She was even more beautiful than he'd remembered. Her golden blonde hair had grown out into long locks and returned to a luster which he couldn't have imagined without seeing her. Beyond her physical appearance, there was something deeper, a contented, happy feeling Josh had never seen in her before. Her face had filled out and she carried a glow, an elegance, and a sense of confidence which caused him to wonder if he was worthy of being with her.

"You look incredible."

She blushed and the color of her cheeks picked up a rosy tint. She shook out her hair and straightened her windblown locks with her fingers.

"Thank you. You look pretty good yourself."

She moved to him, wrapped her arms around him, and squeezed him in her embrace.

"Well, that's the kind of welcome I could get used to." He responded.

"It's really good to see you." She said with a smile.

"It's good to see you too. So what did you have in mind for our date? Seafood? Italian?"

"I've got a surprise for you." She said with a mischievous smile.

"Great, I like surprises."

"You're gonna love this one. Come on."

Taking the passenger spot, he fell back into the leather seat, satisfied with her taking the lead.

"So, when did you get this?" He asked pointing at the car.

"My dad bought it for me."

The fact that she had called Phillip her dad registered with Josh. It told him she was truly on the right track, pushing aside her past and focusing on the future and the people who supported her most.

"It's a nice looking car."

"I love having the top down. It makes me feel so carefree." She looked at him and winked. "Carefree, not reckless."

She pointed the car east and he sat for a moment watching as she drove; the wind whipping the white scarf tied over her hair; her eyes hidden behind the dark shades. She looked like a starlet right out of one of those sixties movies; her energy and vitality making her appear to be a woman well beyond his reach.

Leaving Houston behind, Josh started to wonder just what kind of surprise she had in mind, but as they continued on toward the coast, his suspicions began to develop. There was no doubt Galveston Bay had captured a piece of her heart. He'd seen it in her eyes whenever it entered their conversations.

She reached for the volume on the stereo and he couldn't take his eyes away from her beautifully manicured nails as she turned up the music. He glanced at her and she smiled back, the harmony of a Beach Boys tune lifting into the wind which whipped around them. He closed his eyes and sat back into the seat to relax. He felt her fingers touch the back of his hand, sending electricity though him. He turned his hand over and her fingers grazed against the palm of his hand before she interlaced them with his.

Later as they strolled along the beach just below the sea wall, their hands lingered in a loose, relaxed embrace.

She spoke casually, but meaningfully about how much the beach meant to her.

"I love this place. We came here once when I was a little kid."

She paused, looking out on the horizon.

"You know, it's where I came first when I left home."

She turned to face him and held his hands in hers between the two of them.

"There's this picture my mom has, of her and Daddy Dan. They were in this boat. I used to look at that picture and imagine I was there with them. In my day dreams we were a real family and we took vacations together. Sometimes it seemed so real I would swear I could feel the saltwater spray on my face."

Feeling she had more to say, he kept quiet allowing her to find her thoughts. Her smiling face told him she was experiencing happy memories. Then her face changed and took on a serious look.

"Do you believe every life has a purpose?"

"Yes, I do."

"Even the ones who die tragically like Daddy Dan?"

"Yes, I believe they do. I may not be able to determine what that purpose was, but I think there is one."

"Me, too."

They walked on a few steps before she turned to look at him again.

"I think I know why Daddy Dan died."

He couldn't hide his confusion.

"What do you mean?"

"I think I know the purpose of his life." She said matter-of-factly.

"And what would that be?"

"I think he died so I could find my purpose."

He was trying to follow her train of thought, but he wasn't sure he understood.

"Why did your dad have to die for you to find your purpose?"

"If he hadn't died, I would have had a normal life. I wouldn't have been so confused and I probably wouldn't have become a runaway. And if I hadn't become a runaway, I wouldn't have discovered my purpose."

"And your purpose is?"

"To help other girls."

"But you could have done that even if your dad was alive."

"But I wouldn't have known what they were going through. I had to experience it in order to really relate to them. You can talk to them. You can say all of the right words, but you can't tell them you know what they're going through because you've never experienced it or at least not all of it. I can, and it's all because my dad's life had a purpose. It's the only thing that makes sense."

"You know, God never said it would make sense."

"No, but He also never said it wouldn't." She said confidently.

They spent the evening walking along the Kemah Boardwalk, visiting shops, watching the kids at the stingray aquarium, and taking in the beautiful images around them. Later in the day, they dined above the harbor and watched as the sailboats slipped in and out of the bay. As the day came to a close, they sat with their toes buried into the warm sand, their conversation breaking periodically to take in the sights and sounds of excited gulls diving at the scraps which had washed up upon the beach or been left behind by visitors. Easy laughter punctuated the stories they shared. A sense of romance fell over them as they watched the sun sliding down beyond the horizon like a giant orange tablet dissolving into the water. He felt a warm, laziness envelope him as he watched her speak with animation and he marveled at the power of goodness to triumph over evil.

Sitting in the sand next to her, the rolling waves lapping up on the shore providing background music to her soft voice, he listened as she recanted happy memories from the past. She spoke of visits to the beach as a child, and she told him of the first few days on her own before the magnitude of her decision to leave home had taken its toll.

They spent the first night in separate rooms she'd reserved at a Victorian bed and breakfast overlooking the beach on Galveston Island. They shared breakfast together on a veranda with the whispering sounds of waves sculpting the wet sand, the scent of the sea in the air. As they walked hand in hand along the beach, their footprints trailed behind them only to be erased by the gentle fingers of water moving to and fro along the canvas of the beach. In the evening they once again watched the sun disappear beyond the horizon, while they held each other in the light of a driftwood fire. They spent that night on the beach in each other's arms. She'd planned the whole weekend and though there was a part of him which felt it should have been his idea, he was content to share in her dreams and memories.

As the weekend drew to a close, he found it hard to say goodbye. They were quiet on the trip back to Houston. The sound of the car and the wind kept the silence between them from becoming uneasy. When she pulled up next to his car, he felt his anxiety growing. She sensed it.

"It's okay." She said touching his hand. "It's just for a little while."

He felt embarrassed that she felt the need to reassure him, and she sensed that as well.

"You know, I've learned a lot the past few months. I know I'm younger than you, but in some ways I think I've been forced to mature faster than a lot of people my age. Most of us don't get a second chance; my dad didn't, but for some reason I did. That wouldn't have mattered at all to the old me, but to the new me, it is the most special gift I could ever be given."

As she paused, she moved her thumb gently over the back of his hand. Her eyes met his.

"You've been a very real part of that; one of the most important parts. I had no dreams, no aspirations, and no personal value. I didn't have any purpose, and life didn't much matter, so I was burning it at both ends just to get it over with. Now I know that anything of value is worth waiting for; I don't have to make life to rush by."

She squeezed his hand.

"This is worth waiting for." She said with a confident nod.

He was speechless. He really didn't know what to say to her. He couldn't have said anything anyway; the lump in his throat wouldn't have let the words pass. She was so amazing and he absolutely didn't know why he'd been blessed to fall into her life, but he was smart enough to recognize his blessings for what they were. He struggled to keep from giving in to the emotions trying to overtake him.

"What's wrong? Was it something I said?"

He nodded and cleared his throat.

"Yeah, it was." He whispered.

He took a deep breath.

"I just don't know what I could say to let you know how special I think you are. I wish I could have protected you from the things you have gone through."

She put her finger up to his lips.

"Shh. I wouldn't be who I am now, if I hadn't been where I've been. I'm not saying that I wouldn't have preferred learning what I've learned in a better way, but if that's how it had to happen for me to know what is important, then I guess I have to accept it."

It was the true beginning of a beautiful relationship. It was the moment when he actually understood what had attracted him to her in the first place. Her depth and sincerity; her passion and determination rose to the surface and displayed themselves as the authentic foundations of her personality. Yes, he'd known they were there, but they were buried deep within her at the time. That weekend they were out on display, front and center. She would never hide them again

Twenty-Four

There are things which happen in life, things we simply don't understand. They affect the innocent and the not so innocent. They can be positive or negative, creating lasting impacts which change lives for the better or worse. Sometimes, these events lead us to a greater understanding, and yet, at other times, they may leave us disillusioned and defeated. Quite often, however, the way in which we accept them marks the difference in the outcome.

Who knows why it was necessary for Dan Pearson to die before he ever laid eyes upon his daughter? In fact, who is to say there was a reason at all? Perhaps that event was simply a terrible product of the world in which we live, and all that followed was the process of correcting that ill turn of events. Why was it necessary for Elina to experience what she went through? I don't know, I really don't, but I do know she came through it as a better person than she was before it happened

In my life, I am often faced with trying to find answers to impossible questions, and the honest truth is, sometimes there are no answers, or at least, none that we can understand. Outside of my work in the oilfield, I'm a part-time youth leader, and I minister at the shelter to those who are in need, but even I don't always know why things happen. I guess it all comes down to the phrase Darcy wrote on her mirror that day, "I must have faith, and I must go on."

Elina Pearson became a person who valued the opportunities life presented her. She went back to school and became a student counselor. Her experiences offered her a depth of credibility students seemed to trust. She carries much of her father's ability to grow friendships, and turn the severity of a situation into something more easily accepted. She displays a magnificent beauty, not merely surface beauty, but the rich, life-loving beauty of a person comfortable with who she has become.

Seldom do the two of us speak of what happened. It isn't that Elina seeks to hide from it, but rather, she has chosen to focus on the more positive aspects of life's experiences. Her counseling has helped her a great deal. She has come to grips with the nightmares which haunted her for a significant portion of her childhood, and her relationship with her family is an incredibly uplifting thing for her. In fact, if you were to meet Elina today, you would find it impossible to imagine life had ever dealt her anything but the perfect hand.

To offer some sense of closure, I must say that Elina did identify her attacker, and ol' Hank was sentenced to pay his price. However, for Hank, the price seemed like a ticket to heaven. He wrote often to his friends at the shelter, sharing with them stories of his "three squares a day" and the pleasure of having a dry place to sleep. Of course, he impressed upon them the trials of having a toilet of his own, cable television in his cell, and clean clothes each day. But there was a greater price for Hank to pay, one not determined by the courts or the jurors, nor even by Elina herself. Hank paid with his life at the hands of one of his own. He was found in the shower room, bludgeoned beyond recognition, it seems some of his companions were not fond of rapists.

As for myself, well, I still run the company I started with my step-father and I lead the youth group in that small Oklahoma town where I started out. It is a wonderful little town, and I can't think of a better place to raise a family. Small is good, at least for me. Houston is quite a place, and there are plenty of things to do there, but I prefer the sleepy, quiet of a little one-horse town to the hustle and bustle of city life.

Still, each year I spend a couple of months working at the Shelter on Fannin Street. My other job as an oilfield geologist allows me the funds and the freedom to spend those months helping others. There are so many lives to touch, and sometimes I feel guilty that I actually have the opportunity to leave that place to go home, while there are so many people who cannot. I try to comfort myself by rationalizing that at least I am doing something to help. It is, I suppose, a weakness, but one I choose to accept for the benefit of my family. Yes, my family.

My wife and I have a beautiful daughter. She has her mother's golden hair. Like her mother, she is named after a rose. Our little Elise is a yellow rose, a beautiful reproduction of the wonderful woman I married. Her youthful energy keeps us busy each and every day. I have found the most wonderful moment of the day is when I get to see her snuggled up with her mother. They read together each night at bedtime. Usually, Elise picks the story, but once in a while, her mother tells her the story of The Blemished Rose. It is a wonderful story of redemption and beauty.

It has been nearly seven years since that fateful night in Houston, when I helped to rescue a young woman clinging to life. I am always amazed that of all the things which should come to mind on such a wicked anniversary, my wife chooses to remind me of how God blessed her by sending me to find her. We spend those months in Houston together and Elise stays with her grandparents in Denton.

While I spend my days at the shelter, my wife spends hers talking with the kids on the street, offering them the choice of a better life, encouraging them to think about what brought them there, and what their future holds. Sometimes they listen; sometimes a life is changed, and in that she finds reason to rejoice. My Elina -- my yellow rose -- from a blemished past, has blossomed a wonderful person and an amazing woman.

The Rapture of the Blemished Rose

Once upon a time, in a land far beyond the misty moon, in a world even more magnificently beautiful than our own, there lived a mighty King. He was a King, not because a dusty piece of paper said so, but because he had earned the honor, fighting in great battles against evil and injustice. He was strong and gallant. The blade of his sword was razor sharp, and his swing was firm and true. Yet, despite his brave and fearsome reputation, he was known most for his gentle hand, and his ability to bring to life the most beautiful things. Working with care, he grew beautiful plants and trees; flowers and fruits. Known far and wide as the Master Gardener, he was the keeper of an exquisite and expansive garden of the most amazing plants in the world.

As he walked through the garden, dewdrops glistened in the morning light, reflecting the radiance of dawn like a sprinkling of diamond dust upon the leaves and blades of grass. Stillness hung in the air, and a hush fell over the land, for even the wild things grew quiet when the Master Gardener was near.

There in the garden, he worked to bring to life incredibly beautiful things. He was happy when he was in his garden; gardening was his favorite pastime, and the plants, and bushes, and trees were just as happy to see him. Wherever he walked the green leaves lifted up from the ground, the young buds unfurled their soft petals and opened their sleepy faces, all for just a moment of the master's love and attention.

Moving through the garden, he worked tirelessly. He was patient and caring; and he paid attention to even the smallest detail. There was much to do in such a large and richly filled garden, but the work he loved above all was beginning new life. With a calm and gentle nature, he lovingly helped his young plants to grow, enjoying the beauty of their existence, speaking to them; telling them how much they meant to him, and feeling how much they loved him back.

One day as he walked through the garden, he stopped to look at his latest creation. He held the small plant within his hand, a cutting from a perfect bush. It had been carefully taken, and gently cared for until it could grow on its own. It was beautiful in every way. He gently set it aside and began preparing the ground where it would grow to be a rich and lovely rose bush.

The smell of the dark rich soil lifted up to his nose as the Master Gardener gently turned it over and over with his small spade, preparing the ground to receiving the thread-like roots which would feed the young plant. With each turn of the spade, he lifted and loosened the soil, breaking apart the clumps to form a dark, moist, powdery substance. The tenacious tentacles which formed the roots *of weeds and grasses were carefully removed from the soil, along with rocks and other foreign objects. Into the soil, he mixed food which would help the plant to grow.*

With great attention to detail, the plant was prepared; he spread and separated its roots. With glee in his heart, the gardener replaced the soil, covering the roots and firmly holding the stem so that its top pointed toward the sun. Finally, the gardener offered a drink of water, pure and clear to the young plant. Then he stood back and gazed at his work with a look of satisfaction, pleased with the fruit of his labor.

Scents of lavender, and honeysuckle mingled with the perfume of roses, and jasmine. The crisp odor of evergreen floated in the background, highlighted by the aroma cast aloft by the blossoms of apples, peaches, and pears. The garden was aglow with radiant colors of crimson, gold, and violet. The snow white of the iris played against the orange and yellow glow of the Turk's Cap. Berries of black and blue and red adorned the bushes, plump with sweet and sour juices.

Bees darted to and fro, while butterflies gracefully floated on the gentle breeze which blew the sweet spring smells of the garden, all carrying the fertile dust of pollen to settle in its sacred places, perpetuating life through simple acts. The passage of time held still, neither beginning, nor continuing, nor ending, in this garden of gardens. All was as it ever had been in the garden of the Master Gardener, and yet there was newness, a birth, for the Rose which was once merely a cutting had begun to bloom.

The Gardener walked through his garden, surveying its beauty and order, drinking in the color and splendor, dining on the sweet scents which swept throughout the air. Moisture glistened off the surfaces of the leaves of oak, birch, and walnut. The squirrels feasted on the abundant fruits of the nut trees and the rabbits nibbled at the vegetation. The gardener did not consider them pests nor guests, but rather companions, there to enjoy the beauty and charm of his creation.

Suddenly there came about a chattering from the animals and wild things in the garden, the birds singing like heralds, breaking through the reverence in joyous sounds. Through the foliage of the gateway, a stately figure emerged. He moved swiftly and elegantly toward the gardener. His eyes were bright, yet calm and reassuring.

The gardener turned to face him, an approving smile displayed upon his face.

"Ah, my son. Come and see the young plant. It is just yet preparing to unfurl its young petals."

The son stepped forward to stand next to his father. Together they gazed upon the rose bush, the stems of its branches tipped by tight crimson buds. Again the garden was quiet, but for the conversation of the gardener and his son.

"Father, it has grown magnificently. It promises to be as lovely as the original. In fact, it seems to be very much the same plant, yet in miniature."

The father smiled with satisfaction.

"It is the same plant, for it is but a cutting, a continuation of the perfect beauty from which it came. The life goes on and ever may, as long as it remains unspoiled,

and unblemished; a carrier of the beauty within the design."

Sifting through the branches and leaves of the trees, the sunlight spread into wild, bright beams, each going in its own direction, deflected by leaves, branches, and fruit. In the shadows of the trees little, bright beams sliced through the darkness. Coupled with the quiet drips of moisture from the leaves, the remnant of a morning rain shower, it offered another world-like dimension to the already solemn home of the Master Gardener. Slowly he walked through his garden, surveying his work and the fruits of his toil. He nodded approvingly as he looked around. The garden was much like a living painting. The shapes were filling out nicely, the colors displayed an appealing contrast, and the design was just as he had imagined it would be.

Everything in the garden was perfect; the results of the purest breeding possible. Each apple looked as appealing as the next, their shapes, their colors, and even their taste was exactly the same. Each pear, each peach, apricot, rose, lily, tulip, and mum, all a duplicate of its neighbor. For that is what he loved, creating perfect pieces of living art. Nothing short of excellence could be accepted, not out of pride, but out of love for the beauty of perfection; it was his nature and it would be against his nature for anything less to exist in this place.

As he came upon the young Rose plant, he showed special interest in its progress. The base had grown thick and strong, the stems below the buds were firm and green, the color below the bud, highlighted the crimson red of the buds themselves. From a tiny cutting to a strong plant, it had grown well, maintaining the exact image of plant from which it had been taken. And the buds, well, they were tight little folds of tender petals, just beginning to spring forth into elegant flowers. They were little packages of beauty, with the power to create more life from within them.

And yet, even as he looked upon what seemed to be the potential for great beauty, there was sadness about him. He had seen the signs; with his eye for perfection, there was no mistaking their meaning. It had begun well enough, progressed magnificently, but now there was no doubt that an infection had occurred. The Rose had to go. The blemishes on the petals were duplicated again and again on each crimson bud and they would continue to repeat themselves with the passing of time.

It was discouraging, because he had the greatest love toward all of his creations, and given a choice he would keep each one, but he simply could not allow anything to exist which might somehow fall short of his standard and forever affect the beauty and perfection of the garden. The plant from which the Rose had been taken was itself a work of beauty and it should have produced another perfect plant, but something had happened. A change had occurred, and the young plant was not capable of meeting his expectations. There was simply no other choice, but to remove it from the garden.

The garden itself, despite all of the protection he might offer, was not free from outside influences. The animals roamed freely to and fro, able to enter and leave at their own whim. Any one of them might bring in something from the outside which could have influenced the growth of the plant. The wind which blew gentle *breezes through the garden, helping to spread the pollen and drying the moisture on the leaves which might cause mold or fungus, could have caused the damage as well. Whatever had happened, whatever influence which might be responsible, the effects were the same and the remedy was certain.*

As he lifted the spade, preparing to cut the roots of the plant from the ground, a gentle figure eased up alongside him.

"Father, isn't this the young Rose you so tenderly grew?" He asked with concern.

The gardener nodded.

"Why are you cutting it from the ground?"

The gardener sighed heavily, for his heart was sad.

"My son, something bad has happened to this young plant. Its blooms have blemishes. Its beauty has been destroyed by the ugly stains upon the petals. It must be cut from the ground and thrown out of the garden or else it may spread its disease to others."

The son, who was also an artist, felt sorry for the plant and was sad when he realized that his father felt the need to destroy it.

"Can't something be done? Can it not be repaired in some way?"

The gardener shook his head.

"No my son, the blemish comes from inside the plant. It is not simply some illness which may be treated or healed. The Rose must be destroyed. I will cut it from the earth and burn it; the risk is too great to allow it to remain. All of the other roses in the garden are at stake."

The son looked at the Rose, except for the blemish, the yellow stain upon the petals; it was a source of beauty. The shape of the petals, the tight form of the buds, the deep richness of its crimson color, they were all gorgeous beyond description. The contrast of the crisp green leaves against the dark red of the flower was an artist's delight. The long stems below the flower were strong and sturdy. The plant was truly a marvel, except for the yellow stain.

The son looked up into the eyes of his father and made his plea.

"Father, may I purchase this Rose plant from you. Is there a price I might pay which would keep you from destroying it? I see in this plant, some value."

The father was touched by his son's compassion.

"You understand, my son, it will never produce a beautiful rose? It will never grow the kind of roses which will be desired by others?"

"I understand, but as I have said, I see in it some value. Will you sell it to me?"

The father handed him the spade.

"It is yours for the labor. You may have it if you dig it up, but it cannot stay in the garden."

With that the son smiled, and reached for the spade.

"I understand and I will pay your price."

Outside of his studio, the artist, the son of the Master Gardener, worked diligently. Everything was important; the lighting; the mixing of the colors; the stretching of the canvas. He was committed to his work and eager to paint upon his canvas the beauty of the rose he had purchased with his labor. He had saved the Rose from destruction, but for him that was not enough. There was still more he wished to do.

As the gentle rays of sunlight, which flooded his work area and reflected off the windows of his studio, warmed his back and cast their glow upon the image of the Rose, he moved about with determination and precision. Every detail must be explored; nothing could be missed. Sketching out the image in front of him, he searched with both his eyes and with his heart, allowing his mind to absorb all that he saw. Each turn of a petal, every hint of shadow, and each reflection of light were important to the whole. Anything that might be missed, would take away from the completed work.

The Rose now grew near the gate outside of his studio, surrounded by other gifts from his father's garden. It grew against the wooden fence, and the texture of the wood offered a rugged contrast to the tenderness of the Rose. The blood red flowers seemed suspended in their stages in front of him. Some of them still tightly wound up in their buds, while others spread out their petals to catch the warmth of the sun or the glistening dew of the morning. The sweet aroma of the Rose caught up on the breeze drifted toward him, rewarding his compassion with all it had to offer.

Each day he carried his easel and canvas out to the gate, along with the carefully mixed pallet of colors. His work progressed, changing slightly with the day, or the light, or the growth of the Rose, but never changing in his love or commitment to the task. There were times when he found he must be patient to achieve the desired effect, for not always was the lighting right, when a cloud moved overhead, but he remained in place and waited for the sunlight to return and his Rose to once again bask in its warmth. There were moments when the gentle breeze grew into strong gusts and the Rose swayed under the influence, still he waited.

When at last the work was complete, the artist stood back and admired his work. He smiled, for the rose had fulfilled all of his expectations. Its value had at last been redeemed.

The son searched for just the right frame in which to mount the painting, not just to protect it, but to also add to the beauty of the painting. Satisfied that he had done all he could to produce the finest picture possible, he wrapped the painting and set off to deliver it to its destination.

He arrived at the large home and came to the door just as the master of the home was preparing to exit.

"Sir, I have a gift for you. I have labored for all this time and have produced something of which I am very proud to offer for your pleasure."

The master waved him inside.

"Well, now, let us see what you have produced. I am sure it will be wonderful because I have always been pleased with anything I have seen you do."

The artist unwrapped the painting and held it up for inspection. He could sense the approval. The astonishment in his eyes was deeply gratifying.

"This is by far the greatest painting I have ever seen. Where did you possibly go to find such a wonderful scene to paint?"

The young artist smiled.

"I did not go to any wonderful or beautiful place to find this scene. It was simply painted in the yard of my studio."

The master was confused.

"In the yard of your studio, but this is a large rose garden. I've been to your studio many times. You don't have such a large and beautiful rose garden."

The statement was true, for the artist had taken the single blemished rose bush and from it painted a beautiful garden. In each of the moments the rose had changed, whether under the influence of the sun, the wind, the clouds, or the rain, he had found something special about it to add to his painting. No matter what impact outside sources had on it, to him it remained a thing of beauty and he had included those things in each piece of his painting. The artist had used all of those situations to offer different perspectives and thus transformed the rose into something much larger than it had actually been. He explained all of this to the housemaster and he could see that his work had achieved the desired results.

"What rose is this that you have painted?"

"Why the only rose I have, the blemished rose of course?"

Again the master was confused.

"But where are the blemishes, I see no yellow spots."

"They are no longer there. I purchased the rose, I painted the rose, and I have covered those blemishes to reveal the true beauty of the plant."

The master smiled.

"My son, you have done well. You have redeemed the rose, for it truly is of great value."

And so, the Rose...the Blemished Rose...which was once cast out of the garden, and had been considered flawed and imperfect, became a great work of beauty, and found a very special place inside the Master Gardener's home.

The End

About the Author

C.E. Lemieux, Jr. is the author of Whispers in the Wind, Loving Deacon, There's Something About Henry, The Ladder Climber, and Some Kind of Life. His bittersweet love stories combine descriptive writing and emotional journeys.

A husband and father of four, C.E. makes his home in the Oklahoma Panhandle where several of his stories are set. He is an avid reader of fiction and enjoys baseball, fishing, camping, and traveling.

Connect with C.E.
Twitter: @celemieux
Email: celemieux@lemieuxbooks.com
On Facebook at Whispers in the Wind by C.E. Lemieux, Jr.

Novels by C.E. Lemieux, Jr.

Whispers in the Wind
Loving Deacon
There's Something About Henry
The Ladder Climber
Some Kind of Life
The Blemished Rose

Made in the USA
Charleston, SC
11 March 2016